DARKLING PLAIN

SPECULATIVE FICTION

FICTION

POETRY

NON-FICTION

ARTISTS

DARKLING PLAIN
SPECULATIVE FICTION

Volume 1, Number 1
Summer, 2000

EDITOR & PUBLISHER
David M. Cox

ASSOCIATE EDITOR
J.A. Howard

CONTRIBUTING EDITORS
Eric M. Heideman
Pam Keesey

COVER ARTIST
Philip Hoffman

PRODUCTION
CJ Stone
The Stone Press
651-642-1695

©2000 by David M. Cox for the authors and artists. The opinions expressed herein are not necessarily those of the publisher. All inquiries should be addressed to Darkling Plain, 4804 Laurel Canyon Blvd., Box 506, Valley Village, CA 91607. Darkling Plain *is not* a year-round market—please see contributors guidelines published in this issue. **Subscriptions** *United States:* $20 for a four-issue subscription and $6 for a single copy. *Canada and overseas:* $24 for a four-issue subscription and $7 for a single copy.

FORESHADOWS

When *The Silence of the Lambs* won the Oscar for Best Picture of 1991, an interviewer asked Jodie Foster what she thought of the fact that a horror movie won the coveted award. Her response was, "It's not a horror movie. It's a thriller."

In 1959, when Rod Serling quit writing for the celebrated television show *Playhouse 90* to write for a science-fiction serial he called *The Twilight Zone*, Mike Wallace interviewed him, asking, "…in essence, for the time being and for the foreseeable future, you've given up on writing anything important for television, right?"

A close friend of mine, a highly intelligent, well-educated reader, regularly watches *The X-Files* and even *Buffy The Vampire Slayer* but disdains the genre fiction I like to read (except for mysteries, which she adores).

The sad fact is that many readers place genre fiction in a literary ghetto, scorning it in favor of more "serious" fiction. At other times, it is a guilty pleasure to be privately enjoyed but never admitted in certain circles. In the eyes of many critics (and, I'm sad to say, many publishers and producers,) "sci-fi" is a term applied to pubescent fantasies of phallic spaceships and scantily-clad cosmic beauties, and "horror" is of two kinds: slasher films and *Goosebumps*. They categorize stories based on the unconscious assumption that science fiction absolutely does not belong in the category of good or serious fiction, and anything that is good or serious is clearly something other than genre fiction.

They go so far as to claim that the only good, serious fiction is rooted in the real world and deals with issues relevant to those living in it.

On that point, I couldn't agree more.

Good fiction of any sort is a story with compelling characters and a compelling plot, powerful in the beauty and sophistication of its language, which informs the reader on the experience of being human. It is rooted in the real world and deals with issues relevant to those living in it.

Science fiction—and horror, fantasy, magic realism, and other genres, call it all *speculative* fiction—is fiction which includes an element that does not exist in the real world, something futuristic or otherworldly, fantastic or threatening, ominous or outrageous, as an integral part of the story.

Good speculative fiction does all of these things. It uses this speculative element, whatever it is, to illustrate how science and technology shape our world; to provoke an emotional response that rises from our own experience despite the outlandish subject matter; to spark within us that frisson of fear and the fortitude to face things found only in our own subconscious.

Darkling Plain will bring those stories to you in every issue.

Despite the distinctions that some make between "science" fiction and "literary" fiction, many distinguished literary writers, including Ray Bradbury, Washington Irving, Kurt Vonnegut, Joyce Carol Oates, Edgar Allan Poe, John Updike, Mark Twain, and Thomas Pynchon have all either written science fiction or employed many of its conventions. Twain's *A Connecticut Yankee in King Arthur's Court* has a premise as fantastic as they come. Toni Morrison's *Beloved* is,

among a great many other things, a ghost story. Nathaniel Hawthorne's *The House of the Seven Gables* is likewise. Witness also his story, "Rappaccini's Daughter," a tale of young love poisoned by weird science, which is reprinted only a few pages hence.

Let us not forget plot in the midst of all this talk of literary, character-driven fiction. Without an engaging plot, "character-driven" fiction can devolve into an introspective examination of the author's navel just as quickly as some science fiction stories fall back on the phallic spaceships and oozing, ravenous zombies. Let us also remember that sometimes we *really like* phallic spaceships and oozing, ravenous zombies. Is it impossible that they might appear in a work of serious, character driven fiction?

In any case, I think I can safely say that a great adventure, well-told, is always a classic. You will find those, too, in every issue of this magazine.

Ultimately, good science fiction brings us the best of both worlds, introspection and suspense, insight and adventure. Rooted in reality, it is yet the fiction of dreams. Here is a dream of mine made reality: the very first issue of *Darkling Plain*.

Enjoy.

—David M. Cox

RAPPACCINI'S DAUGHTER

by Nathaniel Hawthorne

A young man, named Giovanni Guasconti, came, very long ago, from the more southern region of Italy, to pursue his studies at the University of Padua. Giovanni, who had but a scanty supply of gold ducats in his pocket, took lodgings in a high and gloomy chamber of an old edifice, which looked not unworthy to have been the palace of a Paduan noble, and which, in fact, exhibited over its entrance the armorial bearings of a family long since extinct. The young stranger, who was not unstudied in the great poem of his country, recollected that one of the ancestors of this family, and perhaps an occupant of this very mansion, had been pictured by Dante as a partaker of the immortal agonies of his Inferno. These reminiscences and associations, together with the tendency to heart-break natural to a young man for the first time out of his native sphere, caused Giovanni to sigh heavily, as he looked around the desolate and ill-furnished apartment.

"Holy Virgin, signor," cried old dame Lisabetta, who, won by the youth's remarkable beauty of person, was kindly endeavoring to give the chamber a habitable air, "what a sigh was that to come out of a young man's heart! Do you find this old mansion gloomy? For the love of heaven, then, put your head out of the window, and you will see as bright sunshine as you have left in Naples."

Guasconti mechanically did as the old woman advised, but could not quite agree with her that the Lombard sunshine was as cheerful as that of southern Italy. Such as it was, however, it fell upon a garden beneath the window, and expended its fostering influences on a variety of plants, which seemed to have been cultivated with exceeding care.

"Does this garden belong to the house?" asked Giovanni.

"Heaven forbid, signor!—unless it were fruitful of better pot-herbs than any that

grow there now," answered old Lisabetta. "No; that garden is cultivated by the own hands of Signor Giacomo Rappaccini, the famous Doctor, who, I warrant him, has been heard of as far as Naples. It is said he distils these plants into medicines that are as potent as a charm. Oftentimes you may see the Signor Doctor at work, and perchance the Signora his daughter, too, gathering the strange flowers that grow in the garden."

The old woman had now done what she could for the aspect of the chamber, and, commending the young man to the protection of the saints, took her departure.

Giovanni still found no better occupation than to look down into the garden beneath his window. From its appearance, he judged it to be one of those botanic gardens, which were of earlier date in Padua than elsewhere in Italy, or in the world. Or, not improbably, it might once have been the pleasure-place of an opulent family; for there was the ruin of a marble fountain in the centre, sculptured with rare art, but so wofully shattered that it was impossible to trace the original design from the chaos of remaining fragments. The water, however, continued to gush and sparkle into the sunbeams as cheerfully as ever. A little gurgling sound ascended to the young man's window, and made him feel as if a fountain were an immortal spirit, that sung its song unceasingly, and without heeding the vicissitudes around it; while one century embodied it in marble, and another scattered the perishable garniture on the soil. All about the pool into which the water subsided, grew various plants, that seemed to require a plentiful supply of moisture for the nourishment of gigantic leaves, and, in some instances, flowers gorgeously magnificent. There was one shrub in particular, set in a marble vase in the midst of the pool, that bore a profusion of purple blossoms, each of

which had the lustre and richness of a gem; and the whole together made a show so resplendent that it seemed enough to illuminate the garden, even had there been no sunshine. Every portion of the soil was peopled with plants and herbs, which, if less beautiful, still bore tokens of assiduous care; as if all had their individual virtues, known to the scientific mind that fostered them. Some were placed in urns, rich with old carving, and others in common garden-pots; some crept serpent-like along the ground, or climbed on high, using whatever means of ascent was offered them. One plant had wreathed itself round a statue of Vertumnus, which was thus quite veiled and shrouded in a drapery of hanging foliage, so happily arranged that it might have served a sculptor for a study.

While Giovanni stood at the window, he heard a rustling behind a screen of leaves, and became aware that a person was at work in the garden. His figure soon emerged into view, and showed itself to be that of no common laborer, but a tall, emaciated, sallow, and sickly looking man, dressed in a scholar's garb of black. He was beyond the middle term of life, with gray hair, a thin gray beard, and a face singularly marked with intellect and cultivation, but which could never, even in his more youthful days, have expressed much warmth of heart.

Nothing could exceed the intentness with which this scientific gardener examined every shrub which grew in his path; it seemed as if he was looking into their inmost nature, making observations in regard to their creative essence, and discovering why one leaf grew in this shape, and another in that, and wherefore such and such flowers differed among themselves in hue and perfume. Nevertheless, in spite of the deep intelligence on his part, there was no approach to intimacy between himself and these vegetable existences. On the contrary, he avoided their actual touch, or the direct inhaling of their odors, with a caution that impressed Giovanni most disagreeably; for the man's demeanor was that of one walking among malignant influences, such as savage beasts, or deadly snakes, or evil spirits, which, should he allow them one moment of license, would wreak upon him some terrible fatality. It was strangely frightful to the young man's imagination, to see this air of insecurity in a person cultivating a garden, that most simple and innocent of human toils, and which had been alike the joy and labor of the unfallen parents of the race. Was this garden, then, the Eden of the present world?—and this man, with such a perception of harm in what his own hands caused to grow, was he the Adam?

The distrustful gardener, while plucking away the dead leaves or pruning the too luxuriant growth of the shrubs, defended his hands with a pair of thick gloves. Nor were these his only armor. When, in his walk through the garden, he came to the magnificent plant that hung its purple gems beside the marble fountain, he placed a kind of mask over his mouth and nostrils, as if all this beauty did but conceal a deadlier malice. But finding his task still too dangerous, he drew back, removed the mask, and called loudly, but in the infirm voice of a person affected with inward disease:

"Beatrice!—Beatrice!"

"Here am I, my father! What would you?" cried a rich and youthful voice from the window of the opposite house; a voice as rich as a tropical sunset, and which made Giovanni, though he knew not why, think of deep hues of purple or crimson, and of perfumes heavily delectable.—"Are you in the garden?"

"Yes, Beatrice," answered the gardener, "and I need your help."

Soon there emerged from under a sculptured portal the figure of a young girl, arrayed with as much richness of taste as the most splendid of the flowers, beautiful as the day, and with a bloom so deep and vivid that one shade more would have been too much. She looked redundant with life, health, and energy; all of which attributes were bound down and compressed, as it were, and girdled tensely, in their luxuriance, by her virgin zone. Yet Giovanni's fancy must have grown morbid, while he looked down into the garden; for the impression which the fair stranger made upon him was as if here were another flower, the human sister of those vegetable ones, as beautiful as they—more beautiful than the richest of them—but still to be touched only with a glove, nor to be approached without a mask. As Beatrice came down the garden-path, it was observable that she handled and inhaled the odor of several of the plants, which her father had most sedulously avoided.

"Here, Beatrice," said the latter,—"see how many needful offices require to be done to our chief treasure. Yet, shattered as I am, my life might pay the penalty of approaching it so closely as circumstances demand. Henceforth, I fear, this plant must be consigned to your sole charge."

"And gladly will I undertake it," cried again the rich tones of the young lady, as she bent towards the magnificent plant, and opened her arms as if to embrace it. "Yes, my sister, my splendor, it shall be Beatrice's task to nurse and serve thee; and thou shalt reward her with thy kisses and perfume breath, which to her is as the breath of life!"

Then, with all the tenderness in her manner that was so strikingly expressed in her words, she busied herself with such attentions as the plant seemed to require; and Giovanni, at his lofty window, rubbed his eyes, and almost doubted whether it were a girl tending her favorite flower, or one sister performing the duties of affection to another. The scene soon terminated. Whether Doctor Rappaccini had finished his labors in the garden, or that his watchful eye had caught the stranger's face, he now took his daughter's arm and retired. Night was already closing in; oppressive exhalations seemed to proceed from the plants, and steal upward past the open window; and Giovanni, closing the lattice, went to his couch, and dreamed of a rich flower and beautiful girl. Flower and maiden were different and yet the same, and fraught with some strange peril in either shape.

But there is an influence in the light of morning that tends to rectify whatever errors of fancy, or even of judgment, we may have incurred during the sun's decline, or among the shadows of the night, or in the less wholesome glow of moonshine. Giovanni's first movement on starting from sleep, was to throw open the window, and gaze down into the garden which his dreams had made so fertile of mysteries. He was surprised, and a little ashamed, to find how real and matter-of-fact an affair it proved to be, in the first rays of the sun, which gilded the dew-drops that hung upon leaf and blossom, and, while giving a brighter beauty to each rare flower, brought everything within the limits of ordinary experience. The young man rejoiced, that, in the heart of the barren city, he had the privilege of overlooking this spot of lovely and luxuriant vegetation. It would serve, he said to himself, as a symbolic language, to keep him in communion with Nature. Neither the sickly and thought-worn Doctor Giacomo Rappaccini, it is true, nor his brilliant daughter, were now visible; so that Giovanni could not determine how much of the singularity which he attributed to both, was due to their

own qualities, and how much to his wonder-working fancy. But he was inclined to take a most rational view of the whole matter.

In the course of the day, he paid his respects to Signor Pietro Baglioni, Professor of Medicine in the University, a physician of eminent repute, to whom Giovanni had brought a letter of introduction. The Professor was an elderly personage, apparently of genial nature, and habits that might almost be called jovial; he kept the young man to dinner, and made himself very agreeable by the freedom and liveliness of his conversation, especially when warmed by a flask or two of Tuscan wine. Giovanni, conceiving that men of science, inhabitants of the same city, must needs be on familiar terms with one another, took an opportunity to mention the name of Doctor Rappaccini. But the Professor did not respond with so much cordiality as he had anticipated.

"Ill would it become a teacher of the divine art of medicine," said Professor Pietro Baglioni, in answer to a question of Giovanni, "to withhold due and well-considered praise of a physician so eminently skilled as Rappaccini. But, on the other hand, I should answer it but scantily to my conscience, were I to permit a worthy youth like yourself, Signor Giovanni, the son of an ancient friend, to imbibe erroneous ideas respecting a man who might hereafter chance to hold your life and death in his hands. The truth is, our worshipful Doctor Rappaccini has as much science as any member of the faculty—with perhaps one single exception—in Padua, or all Italy. But there are certain grave objections to his professional character."

"And what are they?" asked the young man.

"Has my friend Giovanni any disease of body or heart, that he is so inquisitive about physicians?" said the Professor, with a smile.

"But as for Rappaccini, it is said of him—and I, who know the man well, can answer for its truth—that he cares infinitely more for science than for mankind. His patients are interesting to him only as subjects for some new experiment. He would sacrifice human life, his own among the rest, or whatever else was dearest to him, for the sake of adding so much as a grain of mustard-seed to the great heap of his accumulated knowledge."

"Methinks he is an awful man, indeed," remarked Guasconti, mentally recalling the cold and purely intellectual aspect of Rappaccini. "And yet, worshipful Professor, is it not a noble spirit? Are there many men capable of so spiritual a love of science?"

"God forbid," answered the Professor, somewhat testily—"at least, unless they take sounder views of the healing art than those adopted by Rappaccini. It is his theory, that all medicinal virtues are comprised within those substances which we term vegetable poisons. These he cultivates with his own hands, and is said even to have produced new varieties of poison, more horribly deleterious than Nature, without the assistance of this learned person, would ever have plagued the world withal. That the Signor Doctor does less mischief than might be expected, with such dangerous substances, is undeniable. Now and then, it must be owned, he has effected—or seemed to effect—a marvellous cure. But, to tell you my private mind, Signor Giovanni, he should receive little credit for such instances of success—they being probably the work of chance—but should be held strictly accountable for his failures, which may justly be considered his own work."

The youth might have taken Baglioni's opinions with many grains of allowance, had he known that there was a professional warfare of long continuance between him and Doctor Rappaccini, in which the latter was generally thought to have gained the advantage. If the reader be inclined to judge for himself, we refer him to certain black-letter tracts on both sides, preserved in the medical department of the University of Padua.

"I know not, most learned Professor," returned Giovanni, after musing on what had been said of Rappaccini's exclusive zeal for science—"I know not how dearly this physician may love his art; but surely there is one object more dear to him. He has a daughter."

"Aha!" cried the Professor with a laugh. "So now our friend Giovanni's secret is out. You have heard of this daughter, whom all the young men in Padua are wild about, though not half a dozen have ever had the good hap to see her face. I know little of the Signora Beatrice, save that Rappaccini is said to have instructed her deeply in his science, and that, young and beautiful as fame reports her, she is already qualified to fill a professor's chair. Perchance her father destines her for mine! Other absurd rumors there be, not worth talking about, or listening to. So now, Signor Giovanni, drink off your glass of Lacryma."

Guasconti returned to his lodgings somewhat heated with the wine he had quaffed, and which caused his brain to swim with strange fantasies in reference to Doctor Rappaccini and the beautiful Beatrice. On his way, happening to pass by a florist's, he bought a fresh bouquet of flowers.

Ascending to his chamber, he seated himself near the window, but within the shadow thrown by the depth of the wall, so that he could look down into the garden with little risk of being discovered. All beneath his eye was a solitude. The strange plants were basking in the sunshine, and now and then nodding gently to one another, as if in acknowledgment of sympathy and kindred. In the midst, by the shattered fountain, grew the magnificent shrub, with its purple gems clustering all over it; they glowed in the air, and gleamed back again out of the depths of the pool, which thus seemed to overflow with colored radiance from the rich reflection that was steeped in it. At first, as we have said, the garden was a solitude. Soon, however,—as Giovanni had half hoped, half feared, would be the case,— a figure appeared beneath the antique sculptured portal, and came down between the rows of plants, inhaling their various perfumes, as if she were one of those beings of old classic fable, that lived upon sweet odors. On again beholding Beatrice, the young man was even startled to perceive how much her beauty exceeded his recollection of it; so brilliant, so vivid in its character, that she glowed amid the sunlight, and, as Giovanni whispered to himself, positively illuminated the more shadowy intervals of the garden path. Her face being now more revealed than on the former occasion, he was struck by its expression of simplicity and sweetness; qualities that had not entered into his idea of her character, and which made him ask anew, what manner of mortal she might be. Nor did he fail again to observe, or imagine, an analogy between the beautiful girl and the gorgeous shrub that hung its gem-like flowers over the fountain; a resemblance which Beatrice seemed to have indulged a fantastic humor in heightening, both by the arrangement of her dress and the selection of its hues.

Approaching the shrub, she threw open her arms, as with a passionate ardor, and drew its branches into an intimate embrace; so intimate, that her features were hidden in its leafy bosom, and her glistening ringlets all intermingled with the flowers.

"Give me thy breath, my sister," exclaimed Beatrice; "for I am faint with common air! And give me this flower of thine, which I separate with gentlest fingers from the stem, and place it close beside my heart."

With these words, the beautiful daughter of Rappaccini plucked one of the richest blossoms of the shrub, and was about to fasten it in her bosom. But now, unless Giovanni's draughts of wine had bewildered his senses, a singular incident occurred. A small orange colored reptile, of the lizard or chameleon species, chanced to be creeping along the path, just at the feet of Beatrice. It appeared to Giovanni—but, at the distance from which he gazed, he could scarcely have seen anything so minute—it appeared to him, however, that a drop or two of moisture from the broken stem of the flower descended upon the lizard's head. For an instant, the reptile contorted itself violently, and then lay motionless in the sunshine. Beatrice observed this remarkable phenomenon, and crossed herself, sadly, but without surprise; nor did she therefore hesitate to arrange the fatal flower in her bosom. There it blushed, and almost glimmered with the dazzling effect of a precious stone, adding to her dress and aspect the one appropriate charm, which nothing else in the world could have supplied. But Giovanni, out of the shadow of his window, bent forward and shrank back, and murmured and trembled.

"Am I awake? Have I my senses?" said he to himself. "What is this being?—beautiful, shall I call her?—or inexpressibly terrible?"

Beatrice now strayed carelessly through the garden, approaching closer beneath Giovanni's window, so that he was compelled to thrust his head quite out of its concealment, in order to gratify the intense and painful curiosity which she excited. At this moment, there came a beautiful insect over the garden wall; it had perhaps wandered through the city and found no flowers nor verdure among those antique haunts of men, until the heavy perfumes of Doctor Rappaccini's shrubs had lured it from afar. Without alighting on the flowers, this winged brightness seemed to be attracted by Beatrice, and lingered in the air and fluttered about her head. Now here it could not be but that Giovanni Guasconti's eyes deceived him. Be that as it might, he fancied that while Beatrice was gazing at the insect with childish delight, it grew faint and fell at her feet;—its bright wings shivered; it was dead—from no cause that he could discern, unless it were the atmosphere of her breath. Again Beatrice crossed herself and sighed heavily, as she bent over the dead insect.

An impulsive movement of Giovanni drew her eyes to the window. There she beheld the beautiful head of the young man—rather a Grecian than an Italian head, with fair, regular features, and a glistening of gold among his ringlets—gazing down upon her like a being that hovered in mid-air. Scarcely knowing what he did, Giovanni threw down the bouquet which he had hitherto held in his hand.

"Signora," said he, "there are pure and healthful flowers. Wear them for the sake of Giovanni Guasconti!"

"Thanks, Signor," replied Beatrice, with her rich voice that came forth as it were like a gush of music; and with a mirthful expression half childish and half woman-like. "I accept your gift, and would fain recompense it with this precious purple flower; but if I toss it into the air, it will not reach you. So Signor Guasconti must even content himself with my thanks."

She lifted the bouquet from the ground, and then as if inwardly ashamed at having stepped aside from her maidenly reserve to respond to a stranger's greeting, passed swiftly homeward through the garden. But, few as the moments were, it seemed to Giovanni when she was on the point of vanishing beneath the sculptured portal, that his beautiful bouquet was already beginning to wither in her grasp. It was an idle thought; there could be no possibility of distinguishing a faded flower from a fresh one, at so great a distance.

For many days after this incident, the young man avoided the window that looked into Doctor Rappaccini's garden, as if something ugly and monstrous would have blasted his eye-sight, had he been betrayed into a glance. He felt conscious of having put himself, to a certain extent, within the influence of an unintelligible power, by the communication which he had opened with Beatrice. The wisest course would have been, if his heart were in any real danger, to quit his lodgings and Padua itself, at once; the next wiser, to have accustomed himself, as far as possible, to the familiar and day-light view of Beatrice; thus bringing her rigidly and systematically within the limits of ordinary experience. Least of all, while avoiding her sight, should Giovanni have remained so near this extraordinary being, that the proximity and possibility even of intercourse, should give a kind of substance and reality to the wild vagaries which his imagination ran riot continually in producing. Guasconti had not a deep heart—or at all events, its depths were not sounded now—but he had a quick fancy, and an ardent southern temperament, which rose every instant to a higher fever-pitch. Whether or no Beatrice possessed those terrible attributes—that fatal breath—the affinity with those so beautiful and deadly flowers—which were indicated by what Giovanni had witnessed, she had at least instilled a fierce and subtle poison into his system. It was not love, although her rich beauty was a madness to him; nor horror, even while he fancied her spirit to be imbued with the same baneful essence that seemed to pervade her physical frame; but a wild offspring of both love and horror that had each parent in it, and burned like one and shivered like the other. Giovanni knew not what to dread; still less did he know what to hope; yet hope and dread kept a continual warfare in his breast, alternately vanquishing one another and starting up afresh to renew the contest. Blessed are all simple emotions, be they dark or bright! It is the lurid intermixture of the two that produces the illuminating blaze of the infernal regions.

Sometimes he endeavored to assuage the fever of his spirit by a rapid walk through the streets of Padua, or beyond its gates; his footsteps kept time with the throbbings of his brain, so that the walk was apt to accelerate itself to a race. One day, he found himself arrested; his arm was seized by a portly personage who had turned back on recognizing the young man, and expended much breath in overtaking him.

"Signor Giovanni!—stay, my young friend!" —cried he. "Have you forgotten me? That might well be the case, if I were as much altered as yourself."

It was Baglioni, whom Giovanni had avoided, ever since their first meeting, from a doubt that the Professor's sagacity would look too deeply into his secrets. Endeavoring to recover himself, he stared forth wildly from his inner world into the outer one, and spoke like a man in a dream.

"Yes; I am Giovanni Guasconti. You are Professor Pietro Baglioni. Now let me pass!"

"Not yet—not yet, Signor Giovanni Guasconti," said the Professor, smiling, but at the same time scrutinizing the youth with an earnest glance. "What, did I grow up side by side with your father, and shall his son pass me like a stranger, in these old streets of Padua? Stand still, Signor Giovanni; for we must have a word or two before we part."

"Speedily, then, most worshipful Professor, speedily!" said Giovanni, with feverish impatience. "Does not your worship see that I am in haste?"

Now, while he was speaking, there came a man in black along the street, stooping and moving feebly, like a person in inferior health. His face was all overspread with a most sickly and sallow hue, but yet so pervaded with an expression of piercing and active intellect, that an observer might easily have overlooked the merely physical attributes, and have seen only this wonderful energy. As he passed, this person exchanged a cold and distant salutation with Baglioni, but fixed his eyes upon Giovanni with an intentness that seemed to bring out whatever was within him worthy of notice. Nevertheless, there was a peculiar quietness in the look, as if taking merely a speculative, not a human interest, in the young man.

"It is Doctor Rappaccini!" whispered the Professor, when the stranger had passed.— "Has he ever seen your face before?"

"Not that I know," answered Giovanni, starting at the name.

"He has seen you!—he must have seen you!" said Baglioni, hastily. "For some purpose or other, this man of science is making a study of you. I know that look of his! It is the same that coldly illuminates his face, as he bends over a bird, a mouse, or a butterfly, which, in pursuance of some experiment, he has killed by the perfume of a flower;—a look as deep as Nature itself, but without Nature's warmth of love. Signor Giovanni, I will stake my life upon it, you are the subject of one of Rappaccini's experiments!"

"Will you make a fool of me?" cried Giovanni, passionately. "That, Signor Professor, were an untoward experiment."

"Patience, patience!" replied the imperturbable Professor. "I tell thee, my poor Giovanni, that Rappaccini has a scientific interest in thee. Thou hast fallen into fearful hands! And the Signora Beatrice? What part does she act in this mystery?"

But Guasconti, finding Baglioni's pertinacity intolerable, here broke away, and was gone before the Professor could again seize his arm. He looked after the young man intently, and shook his head.

"This must not be," said Baglioni to himself. "The youth is the son of my old friend, and shall not come to any harm from which the arcana of medical science can preserve him. Besides, it is too insufferable an impertinence in Rappaccini thus to snatch the lad out of my own hands, as I may say, and make use of him for his infernal experiments. This daughter of his! It shall be looked to. Perchance, most learned Rappaccini, I may foil you where you little dream of it!"

Meanwhile, Giovanni had pursued a circuitous route, and at length found himself at the door of his lodgings. As he crossed the threshold, he was met by old Lisabetta, who smirked and smiled, and was evidently desirous to attract his attention; vainly, however, as the ebullition of his feelings had momentarily subsided into a cold and dull vacuity. He turned his eyes full upon the withered face that was puckering itself into a smile, but seemed to behold it not. The old dame, therefore, laid her grasp upon his cloak.

"Signor!—Signor!" whispered she, still with a smile over the whole breadth of her visage, so that it looked not unlike a grotesque carving in wood, darkened by centuries—"Listen, Signor! There is a private entrance into the garden!"

"What do you say?" exclaimed Giovanni, turning quickly about, as if an inanimate thing should start into feverish life.—"A private entrance into Doctor Rappaccini's garden!"

"Hush! hush!—not so loud!" whispered Lisabetta, putting her hand over his mouth. "Yes; into the worshipful Doctor's garden, where you may see all his fine shrubbery. Many a young man in Padua would give gold to be admitted among those flowers."

Giovanni put a piece of gold into her hand.

"Show me the way," said he.

A surmise, probably excited by his conversation with Baglioni, crossed his mind, that this interposition of old Lisabetta might perchance be connected with the intrigue, whatever were its nature, in which the Professor seemed to suppose that Doctor Rappaccini was involving him. But such a suspicion, though it disturbed Giovanni, was inadequate to restrain him. The instant he was aware of the possibility of approaching Beatrice, it seemed an absolute necessity of his existence to do so. It mattered not whether she were angel or demon; he was irrevocably within her sphere, and must obey the law that whirled him onward, in ever lessening circles, towards a result which he did not attempt to foreshadow. And yet, strange to say, there came across him a sudden doubt, whether this intense interest on his part were not delusory—whether it were really of so deep and positive a nature as to justify him in now thrusting himself into an incalculable position—whether it were not merely the fantasy of a young man's brain, only slightly, or not at all, connected with his heart!

He paused—hesitated—turned half about—but again went on. His withered guide led him along several obscure passages, and finally undid a door, through which, as it was opened, there came the sight and sound of rustling leaves, with the

broken sunshine glimmering among them. Giovanni stepped forth, and forcing himself through the entanglement of a shrub that wreathed its tendrils over the hidden entrance, he stood beneath his own window, in the open area of Doctor Rappaccini's garden.

How often is it the case, that, when impossibilities have come to pass, and dreams have condensed their misty substance into tangible realities, we find ourselves calm, and even coldly self-possessed, amid circumstances which it would have been a delirium of joy or agony to anticipate! Fate delights to thwart us thus. Passion will choose his own time to rush upon the scene, and lingers sluggishly behind, when an appropriate adjustment of events would seem to summon his appearance. So was it now with Giovanni. Day after day, his pulses had throbbed with feverish blood, at the improbable idea of an interview with Beatrice, and of standing with her, face to face, in this very garden, basking in the oriental sunshine of her beauty, and snatching from her full gaze the mystery which he deemed the riddle of his own existence. But now there was a singular and untimely equanimity within his breast. He threw a glance around the garden to discover if Beatrice or her father were present, and perceiving that he was alone, began a critical observation of the plants.

The aspect of one and all of them dissatisfied him; their gorgeousness seemed fierce, passionate, and even unnatural. There was hardly an individual shrub which a wanderer, straying by himself through a forest, would not have been startled to find growing wild, as if an unearthly face had glared at him out of the thicket. Several, also, would have shocked a delicate instinct by an appearance of artificialness, indicating that there had been such commixture, and, as it were, adultery of various vegetable species, that the production was no longer of God's making, but the monstrous offspring of man's depraved fancy, glowing with only an evil mockery of beauty. They were probably the result of experiment, which, in one or two cases, had succeeded in mingling plants individually lovely into a compound possessing the questionable and ominous character that distinguished the whole growth of the garden. In fine, Giovanni recognized but two or three plants in the collection, and those of a kind that he well knew to be poisonous. While busy with these contemplations, he heard the rustling of a silken garment, and turning, beheld Beatrice emerging from beneath the sculptured portal.

Giovanni had not considered with himself what should be his deportment; whether he should apologize for his intrusion into the garden, or assume that he was there with the privity, at least, if not by the desire, of Doctor Rappaccini or his daughter. But Beatrice's manner placed him at his ease, though leaving him still in doubt by what agency he had gained admittance. She came lightly along the path; and met him near the broken fountain. There was surprise in her face, but brightened by a simple and kind expression of pleasure.

"You are a connoisseur in flowers, Signor," said Beatrice with a smile, alluding to the bouquet which he had flung her from the window. "It is no marvel, therefore, if the sight of my father's rare collection has tempted you to take a nearer view. If he were here, he could tell you many strange and interesting facts as to the nature and habits of these shrubs, for he has spent a lifetime in such studies, and this garden is his world."

"And yourself, lady"—observed Giovanni—"if fame says true—you, likewise, are deeply skilled in the virtues indicated by these rich blossoms, and these spicy perfumes. Would you deign to be my instructress, I should prove an apter scholar than under Signor Rappaccini himself."

"Are there such idle rumors?" asked Beatrice, with the music of a pleasant laugh. "Do people say that I am skilled in my father's science of plants? What a jest is there! No; though I have grown up among these flowers, I know no more of them than their hues and perfume; and sometimes, methinks I would fain rid myself of even that small knowledge. There are many flowers here, and those not the least brilliant, that shock and offend me, when they meet my eye. But, pray, Signor, do not believe these stories about my science. Believe nothing of me save what you see with your own eyes."

"And must I believe all that I have seen with my own eyes?" asked Giovanni pointedly, while the recollection of former scenes made him shrink. "No, Signora, you demand too little of me. Bid me believe nothing, save what comes from your own lips."

It would appear that Beatrice understood him. There came a deep flush to her cheek; but she looked full into Giovanni's eyes, and responded to his gaze of uneasy suspicion with a queen-like haughtiness.

"I do so bid you, Signor!" she replied. "Forget whatever you may have fancied in regard to me. If true to the outward senses, still it may be false in its essence. But the words of Beatrice Rappaccini's lips are true from the heart outward. Those you may believe!"

A fervor glowed in her whole aspect, and beamed upon Giovanni's consciousness like the light of truth itself. But while she spoke, there was a fragrance in the atmosphere around her rich and delightful, though evanescent, yet which the young man, from an indefinable reluctance, scarce-

ly dared to draw into his lungs. It might be the odor of the flowers. Could it be Beatrice's breath, which thus embalmed her words with a strange richness, as if by steeping them in her heart? A faintness passed like a shadow over Giovanni, and flitted away; he seemed to gaze through the beautiful girl's eyes into her transparent soul, and felt no more doubt or fear.

The tinge of passion that had colored Beatrice's manner vanished; she became gay, and appeared to derive a pure delight from her communion with the youth, not unlike what the maiden of a lonely island might have felt, conversing with a voyager from the civilized world. Evidently her experience of life had been confined within the limits of that garden. She talked now about matters as simple as the day-light or summer-clouds, and now asked questions in reference to the city, or Giovanni's distant home, his friends, his mother, and his sisters; questions indicating such seclusion, and such lack of familiarity with modes and forms, that Giovanni responded as if to an infant. Her spirit gushed out before him like a fresh rill, that was just catching its first glimpse of the sunlight, and wondering, at the reflections of earth and sky which were flung into its bosom. There came thoughts, too, from a deep source, and fantasies of a gem-like brilliancy, as if diamonds and rubies sparkled upward among the bubbles of the fountain. Ever and anon, there gleamed across the young man's mind a sense of wonder, that he should be walking side by side with the being who had so wrought upon his imagination—whom he had idealized in such hues of terror—in whom he had positively witnessed such manifestations of dreadful attributes—that he should be conversing with Beatrice like a brother, and should find her so human and so maiden-like. But such reflections were only momentary; the effect of her character was too real, not to make itself familiar at once.

In this free intercourse, they had strayed through the garden, and now, after many turns among its avenues, were come to the shattered fountain, beside which grew the magnificent shrub with its treasury of glowing blossoms. A fragrance was diffused from it, which Giovanni recognized as identical with that which he had attributed to Beatrice's breath, but incomparably more powerful. As her eyes fell upon it, Giovanni beheld her press her hand to her bosom, as if her heart were throbbing suddenly and painfully.

"For the first time in my life," murmured she, addressing the shrub, "I had forgotten thee!"

"I remember, Signora," said Giovanni, "that you once promised to reward me with one of these living gems for the bouquet, which I had the happy boldness to fling to your feet. Permit me now to pluck it as a memorial of this interview."

He made a step towards the shrub, with extended hand. But Beatrice darted forward, uttering a shriek that went through his heart like a dagger. She caught his hand, and drew it back with the whole force of her slender figure. Giovanni felt her touch thrilling through his fibres.

"Touch it not!" exclaimed she, in a voice of agony. "Not for thy life! It is fatal!"

Then, hiding her face, she fled from him, and vanished beneath the sculptured portal. As Giovanni followed her with his eyes, he beheld the emaciated figure and pale intelligence of Doctor Rappaccini, who had been watching the scene, he knew not how long, within the shadow of the entrance.

No sooner was Guasconti alone in his chamber, than the image of Beatrice came back to his passionate musings, invested with all the witchery that had been gathering around it ever since his first glimpse of her, and now likewise imbued with a tender warmth of girlish womanhood. She was human: her nature was endowed with all gentle and feminine qualities; she was worthiest to be worshipped; she was capable, surely, on her part, of the height and heroism of love. Those tokens, which he had hitherto considered as proofs of a frightful peculiarity in her physical and moral system, were now either forgotten, or, by the subtle sophistry of passion, transmuted into a golden crown of enchantment, rendering Beatrice the more admirable, by so much as she was the more unique. Whatever had looked ugly, was now beautiful; or, if incapable of such a change, it stole away and hid itself among those shapeless half-ideas, which throng the dim region beyond the daylight of our perfect consciousness. Thus did Giovanni spend the night, nor fell asleep, until the dawn had begun to awake the slumbering flowers in Doctor Rappaccini's garden, whither his dreams doubtless led him. Up rose the sun in his due season, and flinging his beams upon the young man's eyelids, awoke him to a sense of pain. When thoroughly aroused, he became sensible of a burning and tingling agony in his hand—in his right hand—the very hand which Beatrice had grasped in her own, when he was on the point of plucking one of the gem-like flowers. On the back of that hand there was now a purple print, like that of four small fingers, and the likeness of a slender thumb upon his wrist.

Oh, how stubbornly does love—or even that cunning semblance of love which flourishes in the imagination, but strikes no depth of root into the heart—how stubbornly does it hold its faith, until the moment come, when it is doomed to vanish into thin mist! Giovanni wrapt a handkerchief about his hand, and wondered what evil thing had stung him, and soon forgot his pain in a reverie of Beatrice.

After the first interview, a second was in the inevitable course of what we call fate. A third; a fourth; and a meeting with Beatrice in the garden was no longer an incident in Giovanni's daily life, but the whole space in which he might be said to live; for the anticipation and memory of that ecstatic hour made up the remainder. Nor was it otherwise with the daughter of Rappaccini. She watched for the youth's appearance, and flew to his side with confidence as unreserved as if they had been playmates from early infancy—as if they were such playmates still. If, by any unwonted chance, he failed to come at the appointed moment, she stood beneath the window, and sent up the rich sweetness of her tones to float around him in his chamber, and echo and reverberate throughout his heart—"Giovanni! Giovanni! Why tarriest thou? Come down!" And down he hastened into that Eden of poisonous flowers.

But, with all this intimate familiarity, there was still a reserve in Beatrice's demeanor, so rigidly and invariably sustained, that the idea of infringing it scarcely occurred to his imagination. By all appreciable signs, they loved; they had looked love, with eyes that conveyed the holy secret from the depths of one soul into the depths of the other, as if it were too sacred to be whispered by the way; they had even spoken love, in those gushes of passion when their spirits darted forth in articulated breath, like tongues of long-hidden flame; and yet there had been no seal of lips, no clasp of hands, nor any slightest caress, such as love claims and hallows. He had never touched one of the gleaming ringlets of her hair; her garment—so marked was the physical barrier between them—had never been waved

against him by a breeze. On the few occasions when Giovanni had seemed tempted to overstep the limit, Beatrice grew so sad, so stern, and withal wore such a look of desolate separation, shuddering at itself, that not a spoken word was requisite to repel him. At such times, he was startled at the horrible suspicions that rose, monster-like, out of the caverns of his heart, and stared him in the face; his love grew thin and faint as the morning-mist; his doubts alone had substance. But when Beatrice's face brightened again, after the momentary shadow, she was transformed at once from the mysterious, questionable being, whom he had watched with so much awe and horror; she was now the beautiful and unsophisticated girl, whom he felt that his spirit knew with a certainty beyond all other knowledge.

A considerable time had now passed since Giovanni's last meeting with Baglioni. One morning, however, he was disagreeably surprised by a visit from the Professor, whom he had scarcely thought of for whole weeks, and would willingly have forgotten still longer. Given up, as he had long been, to a pervading excitement, he could tolerate no companions, except upon condition of their perfect sympathy with his present state of feeling. Such sympathy was not to be expected from Professor Baglioni.

The visitor chatted carelessly, for a few moments, about the gossip of the city and the University, and then took up another topic.

"I have been reading an old classic author lately," said he, "and met with a story that strangely interested me. Possibly you may remember it. It is of an Indian prince, who sent a beautiful woman as a present to Alexander the Great. She was as lovely as the dawn, and gorgeous as the sunset; but what especially distinguished her was a certain rich perfume in her breath—richer than a garden of Persian roses. Alexander, as was natural to a youthful conqueror, fell in love at first sight with this magnificent stranger. But a certain sage physician, happening to be present, discovered a terrible secret in regard to her."

"And what was that?" asked Giovanni, turning his eyes downward to avoid those of the Professor.

"That this lovely woman," continued Baglioni, with emphasis, "had been nourished with poisons from her birth upward, until her whole nature was so imbued with them, that she herself had become the deadliest poison in existence. Poison was her element of life. With that rich perfume of her breath, she blasted the very air. Her love would have been poison!—her embrace death! Is not this a marvellous tale?"

"A childish fable," answered Giovanni, nervously starting from his chair. "I marvel how your worship finds time to read such nonsense, among your graver studies."

"By the bye," said the Professor, looking uneasily about him, "what singular fragrance is this in your apartment? Is it the perfume of your gloves? It is faint, but delicious, and yet, after all, by no means agreeable. Were I to breathe it long, methinks it would make me ill. It is like the breath of a flower—but I see no flowers in the chamber."

"Nor are there any," replied Giovanni, who had turned pale as the Professor spoke; "nor, I think, is there any fragrance, except in your worship's imagination. Odors, being a sort of element combined of the sensual and the spiritual, are apt to deceive us in this manner. The recollection of a perfume—the bare idea of it—may easily be mistaken for a present reality."

"Aye; but my sober imagination does not often play such tricks," said Baglioni; "and were I to fancy any kind of odor, it would be that of some vile apothecary drug, wherewith my fingers are likely enough to be imbued. Our worshipful friend Rappaccini, as I have heard, tinctures his medicaments with odors richer than those of Araby. Doubtless, likewise, the fair and learned Signora Beatrice would minister to her patients with draughts as sweet as a maiden's breath. But wo to him that sips them!"

Giovanni's face evinced many contending emotions. The tone in which the Professor alluded to the pure and lovely daughter of Rappaccini was a torture to his soul; and yet, the intimation of a view of her character, opposite to his own, gave instantaneous distinctness to a thousand dim suspicions, which now grinned at him like so many demons. But he strove hard to quell them, and to respond to Baglioni with a true lover's perfect faith.

"Signor Professor," said he, "you were my father's friend—perchance, too, it is your purpose to act a friendly part towards his son. I would fain feel nothing towards you save respect and deference. But I pray you to observe, Signor, that there is one subject on which we must not speak. You know not the Signora Beatrice. You cannot, therefore, estimate the wrong—the blasphemy, I may even say—that is offered to her character by a light or injurious word."

"Giovanni!—my poor Giovanni!" answered the Professor, with a calm expression of pity, "I know this wretched girl far better than yourself. You shall hear the truth in respect to the poisoner Rappaccini, and his poisonous daughter. Yes; poisonous as she is beautiful! Listen; for even should you do violence to my gray hairs, it shall not silence me. That old fable of the Indian woman has become a truth, by the deep and deadly science of Rappaccini, and in the person of the lovely Beatrice!"

Giovanni groaned and hid his face.

"Her father," continued Baglioni, "was not restrained by natural affection from offering up his child, in this horrible manner, as the victim of his insane zeal for science. For—let us do him justice—he is as true a man of science as ever distilled his own heart in an alembic. What, then, will be your fate? Beyond a doubt, you are selected as the material of some new experiment. Perhaps the result is to be death—perhaps a fate more awful still! Rappaccini, with what he calls the interest of science before his eyes, will hesitate at nothing."

"It is a dream!" muttered Giovanni to himself, "surely it is a dream!"

"But," resumed the Professor, "be of good cheer, son of my friend! It is not yet too late for the rescue. Possibly, we may even succeed in bringing back this miserable child within the limits of ordinary nature, from which her father's madness has estranged her. Behold this little silver vase! It was wrought by the hands of the renowned Benvenuto Cellini, and is well worthy to be a love-gift to the fairest dame in Italy. But its contents are invaluable. One little sip of this antidote would have rendered the most virulent poisons of the Borgias innocuous. Doubt not that it will be as efficacious against those of Rappaccini. Bestow the vase, and the precious liquid within it, on your Beatrice, and hopefully await the result."

Baglioni laid a small, exquisitely wrought silver phial on the table, and withdrew, leaving what he had said to produce its effect upon the young man's mind.

"We will thwart Rappaccini yet!" thought he, chuckling to himself, as he descended the stairs. "But, let us confess the truth of him, he is a wonderful man!—a wonderful man indeed! A vile empiric, however, in his practice, and therefore not to be tolerated by those who respect the good old rules of the medical profession!"

Throughout Giovanni's whole acquaintance with Beatrice, he had occasionally, as we have said, been haunted by dark surmises as to her character. Yet, so thoroughly had she made herself felt by him as a simple, natural, most affectionate and guileless creature, that the image now held up by Professor Baglioni, looked as strange and incredible, as if it were not in accordance with his own original conception. True, there were ugly recollections connected with his first glimpses of the beautiful girl; he could not quite forget the bouquet that withered in her grasp, and the insect that perished amid the sunny air, by no ostensible agency save the fragrance of her breath. These incidents, however, dissolving in the pure light of her character, had no longer the efficacy of facts, but were acknowledged as mistaken fantasies, by whatever testimony of the senses they might appear to be substantiated. There is something truer and more real, than what we can see with the eyes, and touch with the finger. On such better evidence, had Giovanni founded his confidence in Beatrice, though rather by the necessary force of her high attributes, than by any deep and generous faith on his part. But, now, his spirit was incapable of sustaining itself at the height to which the early enthusiasm of passion had exalted it; he fell down, grovelling among earthly doubts, and defiled therewith the pure whiteness of Beatrice's image. Not that he gave her up; he did but distrust. He resolved to institute some decisive test that should satisfy him, once for all, whether there were those dreadful peculiarities in her physical nature, which could not be supposed to exist without some corresponding monstrosity of soul. His eyes, gazing down afar, might have deceived him as to the lizard, the insect, and the flowers. But if he could witness, at the distance of a few paces, the sudden blight of one fresh and healthful flower in Beatrice's hand, there would be room for no further question. With this idea, he hastened to the florist's, and purchased a bouquet that was still gemmed with the morning dew-drops.

It was now the customary hour of his daily interview with Beatrice. Before descending into the garden, Giovanni failed not to look at his figure in the mirror; a vanity to be expected in a beautiful young man, yet, as displaying itself at that troubled and feverish moment, the token of a certain shallowness of feeling and insincerity of character. He did gaze, however, and said to himself, that his features had never before possessed so rich a grace, nor his eyes such vivacity, nor his cheeks so warm a hue of superabundant life.

"At least," thought he, "her poison has not yet insinuated itself into my system. I am no flower to perish in her grasp!"

With that thought, he turned his eyes on the bouquet, which he had never once laid aside from his hand. A thrill of indefinable horror shot through his frame, on perceiving that those dewy flowers were already beginning to droop; they wore the aspect of things that had been fresh and lovely, yesterday. Giovanni grew white as marble, and stood motionless before the mirror, staring at his own reflection there, as at the likeness of something frightful. He remembered Baglioni's remark about the fragrance that seemed to pervade the chamber. It must have been the poison in his breath! Then he shuddered—shuddered at himself! Recovering from his stupor, he began to watch, with curious eye, a spider that was busily at work, hanging its web from the antique cornice of the apartment, crossing and re-crossing the artful system of interwoven lines, as vigorous and active a spider

as ever dangled from an old ceiling. Giovanni bent towards the insect, and emitted a deep, long breath. The spider suddenly ceased its toil; the web vibrated with a tremor originating in the body of the small artizan. Again Giovanni sent forth a breath, deeper, longer, and imbued with a venomous feeling out of his heart; he knew not whether he were wicked or only desperate. The spider made a convulsive gripe with his limbs, and hung dead across the window.

"Accursed! Accursed!" muttered Giovanni, addressing himself. "Hast thou grown so poisonous, that this deadly insect perishes by thy breath?"

At that moment, a rich, sweet voice came floating up from the garden: "Giovanni! Giovanni! It is past the hour! Why tarriest thou! Come down!"

"Yes," muttered Giovanni again. "She is the only being whom my breath may not slay! Would that it might!"

He rushed down, and in an instant, was standing before the bright and loving eyes of Beatrice. A moment ago, his wrath and despair had been so fierce that he could have desired nothing so much as to wither her by a glance. But, with her actual presence, there came influences which had too real an existence to be at once shaken off; recollections of the delicate and benign power of her feminine nature, which had so often enveloped him in a religious calm; recollections of many a holy and passionate outgush of her heart, when the pure fountain had been unsealed from its depths, and made visible in its transparency to his mental eye; recollections which, had Giovanni known how to estimate them, would have assured him that all this ugly mystery was but an earthly illusion, and that, whatever mist of evil might seem to have gathered over her, the real Beatrice was a heavenly angel. Incapable as he was of such high faith, still her presence had not utterly lost its magic. Giovanni's rage was quelled into an aspect of sullen insensibility. Beatrice, with a quick spiritual sense, immediately felt that there was a gulf of blackness between them, which neither he nor she could pass. They walked on together, sad and silent, and came thus to the marble fountain, and to its pool of water on the ground, in the midst of which grew the shrub that bore gem-like blossoms. Giovanni was affrighted at the eager enjoyment—the appetite, as it were—with which he found himself inhaling the fragrance of the flowers.

"Beatrice," asked he abruptly, "whence came this shrub!"

"My father created it," answered she, with simplicity.

"Created it! created it!" repeated Giovanni. "What mean you, Beatrice?"

"He is a man fearfully acquainted with the secrets of nature," replied Beatrice; "and, at the hour when I first drew breath, this plant sprang from the soil, the offspring of his science, of his intellect, while I was but his earthly child. Approach it not!" continued she, observing with terror that Giovanni was drawing nearer to the shrub. "It has qualities that you little dream of. But I, dearest Giovanni—I grew up and blossomed with the plant, and was nourished with its breath. It was my sister, and I loved it with a human affection: for—alas! hast thou not suspected it? there was an awful doom."

Here Giovanni frowned so darkly upon her that Beatrice paused and trembled. But her faith in his tenderness reassured her, and made her blush that she had doubted for an instant.

"There was an awful doom," she continued,—"the effect of my father's fatal love of science—which estranged me from all society of my kind. Until Heaven sent thee, dearest Giovanni, Oh! how lonely was thy poor Beatrice!"

"Was it a hard doom?" asked Giovanni, fixing his eyes upon her.

"Only of late have I known how hard it was," answered she tenderly. "Oh, yes; but my heart was torpid, and therefore quiet."

Giovanni's rage broke forth from his sullen gloom like a lightning-flash out of a dark cloud.

"Accursed one!" cried he, with venomous scorn and anger. "And finding thy solitude wearisome, thou hast severed me, likewise, from all the warmth of life, and enticed me into thy region of unspeakable horror!"

"Giovanni!" exclaimed Beatrice, turning her large bright eyes upon his face. The force of his words had not found its way into her mind; she was merely thunder-struck.

"Yes, poisonous thing!" repeated Giovanni, beside himself with passion. "Thou hast done it! Thou hast blasted me! Thou hast filled my veins with poison! Thou hast made me as hateful, as ugly, as loathsome and deadly a creature as thyself—a world's wonder of hideous monstrosity! Now—if our breath be happily as fatal to ourselves as to all others—let us join our lips in one kiss of unutterable hatred, and so die!"

"What has befallen me?" murmured Beatrice, with a low moan out of her heart. "Holy Virgin pity me, a poor heartbroken child!"

"Thou! Dost thou pray?" cried Giovanni, still with the same fiendish scorn. "Thy very prayers, as they come from thy lips, taint the atmosphere with death. Yes, yes; let us pray! Let us to church, and dip our fingers in the holy water at the portal! They that come after us will perish as by a pestilence. Let us sign crosses in the air! It will be scattering curses abroad in the likeness of holy symbols!"

"Giovanni," said Beatrice calmly, for her grief was beyond passion, "Why dost thou join thyself with me thus in those terrible words? I, it is true, am the horrible thing thou namest me. But thou!—what hast thou to do, save with one other shudder at my hideous misery, to go forth out of the garden and mingle with thy race, and forget that there ever crawled on earth such a monster as poor Beatrice?"

"Dost thou pretend ignorance?" asked Giovanni, scowling upon her. "Behold! This power have I gained from the pure daughter of Rappaccini!"

There was a swarm of summer-insects flitting through the air, in search of the food promised by the flower-odors of the fatal garden. They circled round Giovanni's head, and were evidently attracted towards him by the same influence which had drawn them, for an instant, within the sphere of several of the shrubs. He sent forth a breath among them, and smiled bitterly at Beatrice, as at least a score of the insects fell dead upon the ground.

"I see it! I see it!" shrieked Beatrice. "It is my father's fatal science? No, no, Giovanni; it was not I! Never, never! I dreamed only to love thee, and be with thee a little time, and so to let thee pass away, leaving but thine image in mine heart. For, Giovanni—believe it—though my body be nourished with poison, my spirit is God's creature, and craves love as its daily food. But my father!—he has united us in this fearful sympathy. Yes; spurn me!—tread upon me!—kill me! Oh, what is death, after such words as thine? But it was not I! Not for a world of bliss would I have done it!"

Giovanni's passion had exhausted itself in its outburst from his lips. There now came across him a sense, mournful, and not without tenderness, of the intimate and peculiar relationship between Beatrice and himself. They stood, as it were, in an utter solitude, which would be made none the less solitary by the densest throng of human life. Ought not, then, the desert of humanity around them to press this insulated pair closer together? If they should be cruel to one another, who was there to be kind to them? Besides, thought Giovanni, might there not still be a hope of his returning within the limits of ordinary nature, and leading Beatrice—the redeemed Beatrice—by the hand? Oh, weak, and selfish, and unworthy spirit, that could dream of an earthly union and earthly happiness as possible, after such deep love had been so bitterly wronged as was Beatrice's love by Giovanni's blighting words! No, no; there could be no such hope. She must pass heavily, with that broken heart, across the borders of Time—she must bathe her hurts in some fount of Paradise, and forget her grief in the light of immortality—and there be well!

But Giovanni did not know it.

"Dear Beatrice," said he, approaching her, while she shrank away, as always at his approach, but now with a different impulse—"dearest Beatrice, our fate is not yet so desperate. Behold! There is a medicine, potent, as a wise physician has assured me, and almost divine in its efficacy. It is composed of ingredients the most opposite to those by which thy awful father has brought this calamity upon thee and me. It is distilled of blessed herbs. Shall we not quaff it together, and thus be purified from evil?"

"Give it me!" said Beatrice, extending her hand to receive the little silver phial which Giovanni took from his bosom. She added, with a peculiar emphasis: "I will drink—but do thou await the result."

She put Baglioni's antidote to her lips; and, at the same moment, the figure of

Rappaccini emerged from the portal, and came slowly towards the marble fountain. As he drew near, the pale man of science seemed to gaze with a triumphant expression at the beautiful youth and maiden, as might an artist who should spend his life in achieving a picture or a group of statuary, and finally be satisfied with his success. He paused—his bent form grew erect with conscious power, he spread out his hand over them, in the attitude of a father imploring a blessing upon his children. But those were the same hands that had thrown poison into the stream of their lives! Giovanni trembled. Beatrice shuddered very nervously, and pressed her hand upon her heart.

"My daughter," said Rappaccini, "thou art no longer lonely in the world! Pluck one of those precious gems from thy sister shrub, and bid thy bridegroom wear it in his bosom. It will not harm him now! My science, and the sympathy between thee and him, have so wrought within his system, that he now stands apart from common men, as thou dost, daughter of my pride and triumph, from ordinary women. Pass on, then, through the world, most dear to one another, and dreadful to all besides!"

"My father," said Beatrice, feebly—and still, as she spoke, she kept her hand upon her heart—"wherefore didst thou inflict this miserable doom upon thy child?"

"Miserable!" exclaimed Rappaccini. "What mean you, foolish girl? Dost thou deem it misery to be endowed with marvellous gifts, against which no power nor strength could avail an enemy? Misery, to be able to quell the mightiest with a breath? Misery, to be as terrible as thou art beautiful? Wouldst thou, then, have preferred the condition of a weak woman, exposed to all evil, and capable of none?"

"I would fain have been loved, not feared," murmured Beatrice, sinking down upon the ground.—"But now it matters not; I am going, father, where the evil, which thou hast striven to mingle with my being, will pass away like a dream—like the fragrance of these poisonous flowers, which will no longer taint my breath among the flowers of Eden. Farewell, Giovanni! Thy words of hatred are like lead within my heart—but they, too, will fall away as I ascend. Oh, was there not, from the first, more poison in thy nature than in mine?"

To Beatrice—so radically had her earthly part been wrought upon by Rappaccini's skill—as poison had been life, so the powerful antidote was death. And thus the poor victim of man's ingenuity and of thwarted nature, and of the fatality that attends all such efforts of perverted wisdom, perished there, at the feet of her father and Giovanni. Just at that moment, Professor Pietro Baglioni looked forth from the window, and called loudly, in a tone of triumph mixed with horror, to the thunder-stricken man of science: "Rappaccini! Rappaccini! And is this the upshot of your experiment?"

THE BLAIR WITCH PROJECTS

Yep, they're the ugly cinderblock buildings
on the corner of Crowley Avenue and 13th St.
See that dreadlocked man on the corner?
after the patrol car goes by, Papa Jim'll try to sell you
a dime mojo bag, or offer up some flying ointment—
first rub's free, second one's a hundred dollars.

Let's go on inside; I know what you want to see.
On Runestone Lane live Ragnar and Tiswady Schwartz
their trailer immolated in that Burning Man disaster
last year, so now they swill cheap mead, get by on SSI.

And in 666 Set Court is little Rose Marie;
an unwed mom whose baby wasn't fathered
by Satan after all—if we can believe the DNA test—
and now she and her infant—hoofed and horned—
are all alone: a wrong right turn on the Left Hand path.

At 24-7 African Powers Circle is Chango George,
who read Tarot cards and made a good living
till he played too much 21 counting major and minor
arcana, and now his loa has to mount a steed
whose knees were broken by the mob.

Saddest of all, perhaps, is this red-haired lady,
in a tiny room on the corner of Pleiades and Grey Way,
who channeled lush blond aliens from Ganymede
until the real aliens showed up—you remember—looking
like Abe Vigoda and trying to sell insurance.

The teenage gangs are terrible. The Crips took on
their rivals not knowing that these Bloods
can fly and bite. And crime is on the rise—
not a quartz crystal left in this part of town.

Still, things will get better. There'll be
a benefit concert, and Cybill Shepherd,
Tori Amos and Eartha Kitt will sing,
stir the cauldron at the soup kitchen—
and donations of beeswax candles, essential oils
and used grimoires are appreciated, especially
during the holiday season, Lugnasadh through Samhain.

—Denise Dumars

RAPPACCINI'S DAUGHTER: A MODERN TALE OF GOTHIC SCIENCE

by Pam Keesey

"Rappaccini's Daughter," like *Frankenstein* before it, is not simply a Gothic tale, but a tale of Gothic science. Nathaniel Hawthorne, a writer of the American Renaissance, was heavily influenced by the Gothic in art and literature. He, and such notables as Edgar Allan Poe and Edith Wharton, contributed a body of work to a style known as American Gothic.

Gothic art and literature is characterized by a romantic attachment to the past, particularly the Middle Ages, a love of mystery and melodrama, the allure of tragic beauty, mysticism leaning toward the supernatural, and a fascination with death. When done poorly, it is formulaic. When done well, it achieves a dark atmosphere and a heightened anxiety perfect for exploring ethical and moral issues.

The Gothic period dates from 1764, with the publication of *The Castle of Otranto*, to about 1820. Despite this rather narrow window, the influence of the Gothic is apparent even today. Jack Sullivan, in *The Penguin Encyclopedia of Horror and the Supernatural*, describes the Gothic as a style that reintroduced "a treasure of literary motifs from European literature or folklore" that have become synonymous with the Gothic style in literature, including the magical cure, the femme fatale, and the specter bride or bridegroom. Hawthorne creates one of the most memorable femme fatales of American literature in "Rappaccini's Daughter," a dark and moody tale of love, ambition, desire, and scientific progress.

The story is set in the distant past and in a faraway place—Padua, Italy. Beatrice is a motherless child whose father, Giacomo Rappaccini, has used her in one of his ongoing experiments from the time she was born. Giovanni Guasconti is a young student, the foreigner/hero of Gothic tradition, while his mentor, Pietro Baglioni, is the voice of convention. We might do well to think of him as "the villagers" that figure so prominently in the great Universal films of the '30s—concerned, but not always in the right.

Giovanni has come to Padua from Naples to pursue his studies and finds lodgings in a medieval building that, in this setting, is the urban equivalent of the dark and gloomy castle. Above the door, he notices the "armorial bearings of a family long since extinct," a family whose ancestors had been portrayed by Dante "as a partaker of the immortal agonies of his Inferno." This is our first suggestion that Giovanni is crossing the threshold into danger. (If this were an episode of *Scooby-Doo*, this is where you'd see the "I'd Turn Back if I Were You" sign posted on a tree.)

From the window of his room, Giovanni catches his first glimpse of Rappaccini's garden and forms his first impressions of the doctor as he works among his creations. The doctor, Giovanni notes, "betrays no warmth" for his many "children." He wears gloves to avoid touching the plants and turns his face to avoid inhaling their odor. His demeanor is of "one walking among malignant influences, such as savage beasts, or deadly snakes, or evil spirits...."

From this same window, Giovanni catches his first glimpse of Beatrice, "a young girl...beautiful as the day, and with a bloom so deep and vivid that one more shade would have been too much." Rappaccini shows somewhat more affection for this flesh and blood child, yet he turns over his most noxious creation to her sole care. Not only does she refer to this "magnificent" plant, flowering with "purple gems," as sister, she also shares with it a family "resemblance." Even her voice makes Giovanni think "deep hues of purple or crimson."

Having established himself, Giovanni seeks out Pietro Baglioni, an old friend of his father's and the teacher who is to be his new mentor. In his quest to know more about the fair Beatrice, Giovanni asks Baglioni what he knows of Rappaccini, a physician Baglioni describes as "eminently skilled." However, he also notes there are "certain grave objections to his professional character" among his colleagues at the university. Rappaccini would, Baglioni intimates, "sacrifice human life, his own among the rest, or whatever else was dearest to him, for the sake of adding so much as a mustard seed to the great heap of his accumulated knowledge."

Hawthorne, having established each of the characters, has also made it considerably clear that each one of them is a flawed witness to the events that have taken—or are about to—take place. Giovanni is young and impetuous, given to flights of fancy; Rappaccini is ambitious and values his work even above his own life; and Baglioni fears both Rappaccini, his professional rival, and his daughter, whom he believes is "qualified to fill a professor's chair" and is destined to replace him.

At first glance, Beatrice is flawless, a beautiful woman devoted to her father and to her father's work. Beneath the beauty, however, Beatrice hides a fatal flaw. She is poisonous. It is notable that Beatrice's flaw is not an egotistical one, as with the men in the story, but a flaw assigned to her by her own father, who has made her deadly to other human beings by infusing her with the poison of one of his creations. Her father's experimentation has turned Beatrice into a literal femme fatale. Unlike the classic femme fatale whose manipulative whims destroy those who love her, Beatrice is innocent and tragic, much like Lulu in *Pandora's Box* (the 1921 film directed by G.W. Pabst and starring Louise Brooks). Beatrice is destroyed not because of her own conniving behavior, but as a result of the actions of the men around her.

This sympathetic treatment of women is not unusual in Hawthorne's literature (a sympathy, I might add, shared with much of Gothic fiction, especially of that written by women). In fact, the American Renaissance coincided with the women's suffrage movement in the United States. Beatrice is one of many sympathetic women characters that Hawthorne portrayed in his writing. Beatrice—like Hester Prynne in *The Scarlet Letter*, Faith in "Young Goodman Brown," and other Hawthorne heroines—suffers because the men in her life project onto her their own fears, desires, and prejudices. She is never treated as an individual in her own right, but as a means to an end. Beatrice is our tragic heroine, our specter bride.

Giovanni, the erstwhile bridegroom, is too young and inexperienced to be our hero. Although he may one day have the experience, insight, and wisdom to be heroic, in his youth he is naïve and self-absorbed. Giovanni, Hawthorne confides, has not "a deep heart—or at all events, its depths were not sounded now." For now, he, like so many other heroes of Gothic tradition (the male protagonists of the novels of the Bronte sisters, for example, or the young Maxim DeWinter of Daphe DuMaurier's *Rebecca*), must suffer a tragedy of his own making to gain the inner wisdom necessary not only to love deeply, but to mirror the self-consciousness so typical of Gothic heroes.

Giovanni's interest in Beatrice is primarily sexual. His ardor may have the appearance of love, but Hawthorne reminds us, time and time again, that Giovanni has neither the wisdom nor the experience to truly love for love's sake. "It was not love," Hawthorne writes, "…but a wild offspring of both love and horror…." Even Giovanni, who believes himself to be in love, is repeatedly struck by a doubt as to whether or not "this intense interest on his part were not

delusory…merely the fantasy of a young man's brain, only slightly or not at all connected with his heart." As he tries to close the physical gap between them, Beatrice asserts her limits, not by word, but by growing "so sad, so stern…that not a spoken word was requisite to repel him." This lack of desire on Beatrice's part to consummate their relationship results in Giovanni's love growing "thin and faint as the morning mist, his doubts alone [having] substance."

When Giovanni comes to understand what has happened to Beatrice and, by consequence, what has happened to him, he is filled with neither compassion nor concern, but with a great deal of anger that he has no problem directing toward Beatrice alone. "Thou hast made me as hateful, as ugly, as loathsome and deadly a creature as thyself—a world's wonder of hideous monstrosity," he proclaims, blaming Beatrice for his condition and showing little concern for hers.

Baglioni, despite his concern for Giovanni and his concerns regarding the ethics of Rappaccini's scientific work, has little compassion for Beatrice, whose scientific talents he fears. We know that Baglioni's critique of Rappaccini is suspect, for Hawthorne has already warned us that there is "a professional warfare of long continuance" between Baglioni and Rappaccini, and that Rappaccini is thought to have gained the advantage. Baglioni's professional jealousy is at the heart of his critique of Rappaccini, and it is not without envy that he regards Rappaccini's innovative approach to his work. When it comes to Baglioni's attention that Rappaccini has designs on the young man, Baglioni sees Beatrice as a vehicle for avenging himself and his investment in Giovanni, proclaiming, "It is too insufferable an impertinence in Rappaccini, thus to snatch the lad out of my own hands….This daughter of his!....Perchance, most learned Rappaccini, I may foil you where you little dream of it!"

Rappaccini, it seems, has created a house of glass, and Baglioni is about to cast his stone.

Rappaccini is a maverick scientist, the kind called "mad" in popular culture. His love of science is legendary among his colleagues to the degree that he is known to care "infinitely more for science than for mankind." There is, it is conceded, a certain nobility to so "spiritual a love of science," but there is danger as well. "[T]he signor doctor does less mischief than might be expected with such dangerous substances," notes Baglioni, but has had some notable failures, as well, that have figured very little in the formation of Rappaccini's reputation.

Rappaccini's madness is suggested by his appearance: "a tall, emaciated, sallow, and sickly-looking man, dressed in a scholar's garb of black. He was beyond the middle term of life, with gray hair, a thin gray beard, and a face singularly marked with intellect and cultivation, but which could never, even in his more youthful days, have expressed much warmth of heart." When Giovanni enters the realm of Rappaccini's attention, it is only with this sort of detached scientific curiosity that Rappaccini is able to acknowledge Giovanni's existence. Baglioni, having stopped Giovanni in the street, notices that Rappaccini has "fixed his eyes upon Giovanni...with a particular quietness in the look, as if taking merely a speculative, not a human, interest in the young man." Rappaccini is unable to see Giovanni as a human being, but only as a specimen to potentially be utilized in one of his experiments.

This is, unfortunately, true of his daughter as well. Rappaccini is "a man fearfully acquainted with the secrets of Nature," Beatrice tells Giovanni, and the plant that is her charge and her father's pride and joy is "the offspring of his science, of his intellect, while I was but his earthly child." She was raised side by side with this plant as a sister and "was nourished with its breath" from her earliest days. She is the embodiment of her father's "fatal love of science," the results of which have made it necessary for her to remain isolated from the rest of the world lest she infect it with her unusual—and deadly—quality.

Realizing that she is forever condemned to the same isolation that Rappaccini has embraced, to be forever separated from her beloved Giovanni, she challenges her father's motives for the first time, asking, "wherefore didst thou inflict this miserable doom upon thy child?" Rappaccini, denying any wrongdoing, insists that his actions were taken entirely with her best interests in mind.

When Beatrice finally acts on her own behalf, taking her fate into her own hands by taking Baglioni's powerful antidote—which, of course, turns out to be the very antithesis of the magic cure—in the hopes of counteracting the poison in her system, one cannot help but feel that Baglioni knew what the result would be. His gleeful accusation, "And is *this* the upshot of your experiment?" suggests his desire to attack Rappaccini indirectly by attacking the "results" of years of scientific experimentation, in other words, by attacking Beatrice herself. Giovanni has made her final hours miserable with his selfish accusations. Baglioni has guaranteed her condition to be fatal. And Rappaccini, in his search for knowledge at any cost, has sacrificed his daughter on the altar of scientific knowledge.

Rappaccini is a brilliant scientist who takes a great deal of pride in the work that he does. His daughter is his sole creation with whom he can share warmth and affection, the only one of his many children who is able to give affection in return. Yet his ambition prevents him from loving this "earthly child" for her own sake, and it is not until he is faced with her death that he is forced to consider the consequences of his work.

Rappaccini has dared to play God in creation. When Giovanni first glimpses Rappaccini at work in his garden, he wonders if this mad man is the "new Adam." Sequestered away behind the walls of his home, Rappaccini, like Adam, works in his garden, a toxic "Eden of the present world," identifying and classifying each plant and its respective characteristics. Unlike Adam, however, Rappaccini has taken it upon himself to not only study and observe the natural world, but to actively intervene and usurp and redirect nature's energy. He believes that "all medicinal virtues are comprised within those substances which we term vegetable poisons." He becomes involved with the creation of new life through plant breeding, giving birth to a "commixture, and, as it were, adultery of various vegetable species...no longer of God's making, but the monstrous offspring of man's depraved fancy...." This is also true of his daughter, a monstrous offspring of plant and animal species. He has taken it upon himself to create this new Eve and has designs to make of Giovanni his new Adam.

Rappaccini's fatal love of science is the cause of Beatrice's death and his own undoing. This fatal love of science consists not only of his deadly experiments, but also of his need to elevate his pursuit of scientific knowledge above all else—above his daughter, above his relationships with colleagues, above ethical considerations, and above the essential integrity of another's humanity. And here we strike at the heart of Gothic science.

Gothic literature, with its sometimes trite emphasis on dark and gloomy castles, forlorn and tragic heroines, and wandering and ineffectual heroes, can fall easily into sensationalism and sentimentality. But these same qualities, in the hands of a skilled writer, establish a mood that enables the author to create a tableau of human imagination, an entrée into the psychological underpinnings of anxiety and dread. Traditionally, the Gothic has relied on the involuntary isolation of the individual to help create that state of anxiety. In Gothic science fiction, however, the scientist has voluntarily isolated himself. Rappaccini's pursuit of power in the guise of knowledge makes him the source of the dread and anxiety—whether in the form of his ambition or the monstrosity he has created—that drives the story.

The rise of Gothic art and literature coincided with the rise of the Industrial Revolution, a time of social change, cultural upheaval, and scientific progress. Advancements in medicine, engineering, and technology posed as many, if not more, questions as they answered. Gothic science fiction gave voice to ethical concerns, questions of pride and ambition, of the danger of playing God by seeking to explain—and effect—the miraculous in merely human terms.

"Rappaccini's Daughter" is a synergistic tale, a story that is much more than a sum of its parts. By tapping into archetypal imagery, Hawthorne created a tale that can be read and reread, each reading bringing with it a different emphasis, each interpretation bringing forth another story within a story. As Gothic science fiction, "Rappaccini's Daughter" is a cautionary tale, an allegory that warns us away from scientific progress without ethical consideration.   -*dp*-

ENTROPY VISION

sees it all falling
apart at the seams of time
split out
like the seat in a worn pair of
genes mutating
a redshift failing of faith in stars
or history's arteries
hardening

heat bleeding
out of each fragile skin capsule
the subtle
erosion of touch

a worm at the heart
of the universe

still hungry.

—Ann K. Schwader

NOCTURNE: NOSTRADAMUS

That old Cassandra catch:

beyond
his only blind event horizon
Michel de Notredame defies
line time in Centuries unblessed
by sweet belief

or quatrains chiming
warning clear as death.

Slipped free in space-time trance
his wormhole
mind turned fate's most frequent flyer
tarnished free will
tin illusions

even bright Apollo never
promised more than that.

—Ann K. Schwader

THICKER THAN WATER

by H. Courreges LeBlanc

"How about some sounds this morning?" Arnaud said, turning on the tone sculptor.

"Not that noise box again? Gimme a break—you know I'm hung over," said Caine, tinkering with the solar electric outboard motor.

"I've got just the thing."

"This is really starting to irritate me."

"Good," said Arnaud, tapping a key repeatedly to increase the tempo. "It's my morning mix. It's supposed to get you going. Pump you up."

"I'll pump you overboard into the swamp if you don't shut that off." Caine gestured overboard. The swamp was still black, but here and there the milky tendrils of Mud-Dri were starting to show up.

"We're here, anyway." What a grouch Caine became when he was hung over. Arnaud shut off the sound and tied the boat to the house's front porch. The house was completely above the water line; bayou Cajuns had been building on stilts for centuries.

A young woman appeared behind the screen door, then vanished. Arnaud got out of the boat and knocked. "Relocation crew. Anybody home?"

"Yeah, we home," came a thin, reedy voice. "You go let the men inside, Julie." It had been a long time since Arnaud had heard that name pronounced Cajun-style, with the accent on the second syllable.

The young woman reappeared, but didn't open the door. She peered at them through the screen, scrutinizing, so Arnaud decided to stare right back. She was worth staring at, too—a real dark-haired Cajun beauty. Her dress had to be older than she was, though.

"You like this dress, eh?" she said with a flip of her hair. "Or maybe you got them x-ray eyes?"

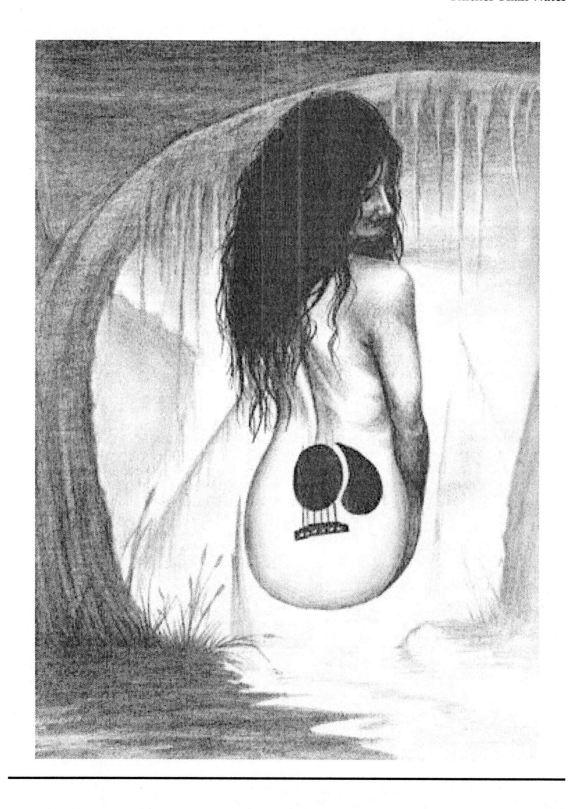

Arnaud, embarrassed, reached for his Corps ID. " 'Scuse me, ma'am. I'm Arnaud Bechet, with the Flood Relocation Corps."

She took his ID card, studied it. "Your name be Bechet, eh?" She pronounced it "bay-shay," instead of "beck-it" as Arnaud had.

"Bechet, ma'am," Arnaud said, correcting her pronunciation. He was no Cajun any more.

She laughed, opening the door. "Eh, marain! Regards cette fou qui ne connais qu'il s'appelles!"

Caine pulled out his translation tablet and started laughing, too. Arnaud was starting to get irritated. "What did you say, ma'am? I didn't understand you."

"Oh, I was telling my auntie what a handsome gentleman you are," she said, laying a soft hand on his arm. Caine laughed even harder. Arnaud snatched the tablet from Caine. It still had the translation on screen: "Hey, godmother! Look at this fool who doesn't even know his own name!"

Arnaud could see the old lady now; his eyes were adjusting to the cabin interior. She sat in an old wooden rocking chair, a shotgun resting in her lap. She was smoking a pipe. "What you want?" she snapped.

"Begging your pardon, ma'am, but is this the LaBas residence?" She nodded, so he handed her the notice. "You're hereby served with your third and final notice. This whole area is slated for the reconstruction of New New Orleans."

She took the paper, not even glancing at it. "So we gotta go, eh?"

"Yes ma'am. Sorry, ma'am. The water was seeded with Mud-Dri crystal a couple of days ago. You don't have much time left." Arnaud was sneaking glances at the cabin. They didn't seem to have electricity, much less net hookups. All the furniture was made

of wood—this stuff, ugly as it was, would fetch a fortune back in civilization.

"We gotta move, then?" She dropped the notice on the floor and relit her pipe. Arnaud said nothing. "Go north, like your grampa did? Live maybe in Nebraska or Minnesota? Forget our native tongue so we can't even say our own name no more? Forget gumbo, jambalaya, étouffée? Maybe when this old lady she want some seafood, you teach her how to make that tuna hot dish?"

She cocked the gun, pointed it at Arnaud. "You get your scrawny ass out o' here, boy."

The girl was laughing harder than ever now. So was Caine, damn him.

"I'll leave, ma'am. I've delivered notice, and that's what I'm here to do. You can paddle out today or walk out next week. It's all the same to me." He turned his back to the old lady. Maybe he couldn't speak the Cajun patois of his ancestors, but he wasn't going to be a coward.

Caine laughed all the way back to the boat. "You got the natives eating out of your hands, Arnaud. They embraced the prodigal son, all right."

"Fat lot of help you were," Arnaud said. "You'd have probably just stood there snickering while the old lady shot me."

"Aw, she wouldn't have shot you. A sweet old lady like that shoot a good Cajun boy like old Arnaud Bechet?"

"Oh, shut up."

They finally gave up on finding a dry spot for camp. They anchored the inflatable pontoon tent to a couple of convenient cypress knees. Arnaud peered through the drooping Spanish moss at the rising moon. In this light, he couldn't see the white streaks of Mud-Dri.

"This place sure is pretty," he said.

"Yeah, if you like mosquitoes," Caine replied, slathering repellent on his arms.

"What a philistine you are. You have no soul."

"Oh, right. I suppose it's Julie's soul you were trying to see through that dress, eh?" Caine chuckled.

"Okay, I admit it," Arnaud said. "I'm attracted to a beautiful woman. I guess that makes me a pervert, eh?"

"You had the hots for auntie, too."

"I don't know why I even listen to you, Caine. You're never serious about anything."

"Always serious about nooky."

"Your problem is that you're a prisoner of your hormones. I can feel my passion, and then channel it through my artistic nature."

"Oh, God, you're not going to break out the noise box again, are you?"

Arnaud didn't dignify that with a reply as he unpacked his tone sculptor.

"You talk about my problems," said Caine. "You're the one with a problem. You and your 'art.' You live in a world of illusion. At least I know the difference between lust and love. But for you, the glorious artiste, every piece of tail is the Mona Lisa."

"Oh, listen to Mister Sensitive! To you, every woman is just a piece of tail!"

Caine grinned as he rummaged through the food box. "Not every one, just the ones you meet on the road. And to them, that's what I am too. We're okay with it; you're the one with the problem. What you want for dinner? Tuna?"

"I bet you like marain's gator piquant more than that tuna," came a female voice from over Arnaud's shoulder.

Arnaud nearly dropped his tone sculptor. Where had Julie come from? How long had she been there? These bayou Cajuns could sneak up on you in their pirogues and you'd never know it.

"You're probably right," Arnaud said, "but she invited me outdoors with her shotgun. Once is enough."

"Oh, she sorry about that. She got a temper, she do. But she like you—she take a shine to you."

"Yeah, Arnaud, she didn't even shoot you," Caine said. "Can't get more affectionate than that."

"Your partner be some kind of smart mouth Yankee," Julie said, unperturbed, glancing at Caine as she paddled away. "But he can come too."

"Mmm, this is good, Mrs. LaBas." Arnaud said around a mouthful. He hadn't tasted anything like it since he was a little boy. The tomato-based broth was peppery and tart, with the taste of seafood. The flavors of childhood stirred the slumbering ghosts within his heart.

"You can call me Miz Lourdes. Gator be good eating, eh?" said the old woman.

"You mean...alligator?" asked Arnaud, turning pale.

"Sure, sure, what you think gator piquant be made with? Chicken?"

"Isn't that kind of dangerous?" asked Caine.

It was Julie who answered. "I shot him this morning on the porch, then grab him quick with the gaff hook before he flop back into the water. No danger, not on the porch. Gator be stupid."

"But alligators are protected!"

"Didn't work," the old woman said.

"He means they're on the endangered list," said Caine. "You're not supposed to hunt them."

"Didn't hunt for him," answered Julie. "He come up on the porch."

"Anyway," the old woman continued, "You mighty tender about this gator, considering you about to kill thousands of gators, plus everything else, presently."

"That's different." Arnaud squirmed. She was right, of course. That part of the job did bother him.

"Ain't no different, son. You need what the gator got, so you kill him. You do it factory-style, not with your hands like this poor little coon-ass girl. We just hungry; you Corps sons of bitches just too damn greedy. Why you pick on us?"

"Yeah," Caine chimed in. "Lay off, Arnaud, she's our hostess." He turned to the old lady. "I'd like some more, if you don't mind."

"You like that gator, n'est-ce pas?" she said. "I give you some of that gator boudin I made, too. Be good lunch for a growing boy. Here, you have some more too, orphan boy." She ladled some more onto Arnaud's plate.

"How'd you know I was an orphan?"

"Marain ain't stupid, cher," Julie said. "You got Creole blood in you, with a name like Arnaud Bechet. Why, I bet you kin to Sidney Bechet!"

"Who's that?" asked Caine.

"New Orleans jazz musician," the old lady said. "Mighty famous among them as not ignorant Yankees."

"I don't know if I'm related to him," Arnaud said, suppressing a smile at the old lady's spunk. "My father died when I was just a baby, and my mama died in '28 during hurricane Virginie."

The old lady's face darkened, and she crossed herself. "That a dark year, boy. Many good people passed on before their time."

"Thirty four hurricanes in one season," Julie said, subdued, and crossed herself too.

"The Lord be mighty angry that year. 'Twerent for his promise to Noah, he kill us all with the flood."

"I was pretty young at the time," Arnaud said. "Maybe three or four. I sat in the attic of our house, watching the water rise through a tiny window. The wind howled so loud it filled the whole world. I could see my mother shouting to me, but I couldn't hear her at all. That was the scariest part, not hearing her."

"Pauvre petit," the old woman said, patting Arnaud's hand.

"Then the roof just peeled back, like the can of sardines we'd had for supper. And the wind snatched me into the air and dropped me miles from home. I remember looking down at mama, watching her watch me as I spun upward." Arnaud noticed he was holding Julie's hand, clutching so tight it must've hurt her. She didn't pull away, though. "I must've passed out, because the next thing I remember was waking up face down on the sidewalk, covered with mud. I wandered for days till I made my way home, and when I got home, I found mama dead."

A silence fell over the table. The old woman finally broke it, saying: "How'd you live? A child that small need someone to watch over him."

Arnaud stared at the floor a long time. Then he sighed and said, "I was taken in by a treasure hunter from New Orleans. Iggy, his name was."

"Yankee?" the old lady asked, not quite masking the scorn in her voice.

Arnaud smiled. "No, he was born and raised in New Orleans, but ran off north for fame and fortune."

"Like you."

Arnaud smiled. "Yeah. My bones are Cajun, but my head is pretty much Yankee."

"That explain a lot," Julie said. "Your blood be torn in half all your days."

"Maybe so," he admitted. "That's also why I'm in the Corps. Iggy was there to help me when I needed it."

"And you run off," Julie said.

"Young folks always got that urge to run," the old lady said. "The foolishness take hold, they let go of all they love."

"That's not it at all," Arnaud said. "I joined the Corps to give back. Besides the ones killed by the floods, there are so many who've been driven from their homes. The Corps is helping to build new homes."

"You ain't helping," the old lady said evenly. "You gonna make it worse. You fill up this swamp with that death jelly. She kill everything, then seize up like concrete. All the swamp become nothing but a banquette."

"A what?" Caine asked.

"Sidewalk. All you crazy Yankees, you chop down the forests, drain the swamp, pave the prairie. God smite the world then, with floods and storms, plagues and quakes, warning you. And how you wanna fix things? More cement. You people crazy."

"But what about all the people displaced by the storms?" asked Arnaud. "Where are they supposed to go?"

"Don't know," the old woman admitted. "But New Orleans, she still there. She be a ghost, but she ain't gone. You can't change the past, can't wipe it away or leave it behind. You build some Yankee suburb on a dead, paved-over swamp, that ain't making nothing no better."

"I don't think you realize how big the housing crisis is," Arnaud said. "It's not just New Orleans. We lost most of our coastal cities—New York, Los Angeles, Boston. Tens of millions of people lost their homes."

"So I gotta lose mine, too?" the old woman said. "This your mighty work, your good deed?" She wheeled to Caine. "You being mighty quiet, Yankee. You be a mis-sionary too? You wanna believe you can help all them people what ain't no kin of yours?"

"Nah," Caine said easily. "I joined the Corps to get the college deal. "My people live in Detroit, they're all okay. The flooding wasn't so bad there. But we're poor. I wanna go to school, be a lawyer, and suck some money from the rich."

The old woman smiled. "You never be a lawyer. You can't lie with a straight face."

"That's okay," he replied. "Rich Yankees are too stupid to know the difference."

Everyone laughed at that, glad to release the tension.

"Julie," the old woman said. "Go get your guitar and play some music for these boys."

"Oh, marain!" Julie yelped, clearly embarrassed.

"Come on, child. You know you play good. You got the gift."

"Yeah," chimed in Caine. "I never heard guitar, but it's gotta be better than Arnaud's music box."

Julie shot a poisonous glare at her aunt, then ran into the other room without a word.

"You play accordion?" the old woman asked, surprised.

"No, ma'am," Arnaud said. "I make tone sculptures."

"What that? Music?"

"Not exactly," Arnaud said.

"You can say that again," Caine said.

Before Arnaud could come up with an adequate retort, Julie returned with her guitar. She stabbed the old woman with another glare, then sat down and began tuning.

He'd seen pictures of guitars, but hadn't realized how beautiful they were. Its body curved seductively in Julie's lap, the pale, streaked wood contrasting Julie's dark braids.

"You like my niece's guitar, boy?" the old woman said, smiling.

"It's very pretty," he said, wincing as she plucked high, hollow harmonics from two strings, turning the pegs until the beat frequencies meshed. The closer the tones were, the worse it sounded—until it was perfect. "Um, what kind is it?"

"Taylor," Julie muttered, still tuning.

"That doesn't sound very Creole," Caine said.

"Nah, they Yankees," the old woman said. "Make a good guitar, though. Single piece maple construction on body make pure tone, skinny neck give you good action. Good mechanicals on pegs too."

"Do they still make them?" Arnaud asked.

The old lady snorted. "Course not. Nobody want real music any more. Too much work to learn to play a actual instrument." She turned to Julie. "You tune that thing yet?"

"Hold your horses," Julie snapped, still tuning. "It be tuned presently. You got no patience, marain. Why you got no patience, old as you are?"

"Ta bouche, it try the patience of a saint, girl. The patience of a saint."

Caine dug his elbow into Arnaud's ribs and grinned. Arnaud ignored him. "You sound like you know quite a bit about guitars, ma'am. Do you play?"

The old woman's face creased. "Not no more, boy. These old hands got no music left in them."

"She got the arthritis," Julie said in a pitiless tone, not looking up.

"I'm sorry," Arnaud said. "You know, you might be interested in the tone sculptor. You don't need much agility to play it—it's mostly conceptual. You can make music without having to move your fingers very quickly."

The old woman smiled. "I do that already with my boom box. Play them CD's."

"You still have a CD player?" Caine asked. "Incredible! I didn't know anyone had a functioning CD player."

"Sure. Work just fine. Had to jury-rig power supply, though. Can't get batteries no more."

"Okay, marain. She tuned now, so you shut up if you want me to play so bad."

The old woman made no reply, but folded her hands in her lap. She's not giving Julie any excuses, thought Arnaud.

"Okay, then." Julie brushed her bangs from across her face. "I start with an old Billie Holiday tune, called 'Strange Fruit.'"

It started so quiet and pretty, Arnaud was caught unprepared by the emotional assault of this song. Mournful chords smoldered with restrained tension. Julie's uninflected, dry voice delivered the lyrics like a newscaster, the melody made only of the meaning of the words—harsh, brutal, unimaginative. These words were too true to ever be spoken; the tune was the only way they could be released. How could someone so young and pretty know suffering so intimately? How could she stand to sing this?

When the song ended, Julie launched into another one. Then another, and another. Sometimes she'd announce the title just before starting. "Jeepers Creepers." "Blue Moon." "Stormy Monday." Many were tunes that his stepfather Iggy had played for him, long forgotten. Each song submerged him deeper into a world that time had washed over. Dimly, he'd hear Caine and the old woman clapping between each song, but he never had time to break through the surface before she drowned him again.

Finally, mercifully, she stopped.

The old woman leaned toward Arnaud. "She mighty good, eh?"

He nodded, still struck mute.

"Wow!" Caine said. "That's really something. Where'd you learn to play this?"

"Taught myself," Julie said, putting the guitar back in its case. "Maybe I go to some Yankee city some day, play my music there."

"You'd never make it," Caine replied. "Nobody wants to hear this old-time stuff. Everything's tone sculpture these days. Tone sculpture and 3D holo."

"I bet I could do that too," she said.

"Sure you could!" Arnaud said. "I'd be glad to show you. Tone sculpture is easy."

"You show her au matin," the old woman said. "Time for you men to go."

"See, this controls the frequency of the notes." Arnaud reached over Julie's shoulder, touching her hand and pointing to the control panel. God, she smelled good. They were on her front porch, the morning sun still not above the cypress tops.

She turned to look at Arnaud, her face inches from his. "Frequency? You mean pitch?"

He could feel the warmth of her breath. Her eyes were so dark, the irises more black than brown.

"You awake, orphan boy?" Julie teasingly nudged his shoulder.

"Oh, sorry," Arnaud said. "No, on this screen frequency refers to how often the notes occur. The notes themselves are derived from random numbers, as filtered here." He pointed at the button for the filter selector, and Julie slid her hand under his to press the button.

"Filtered how?"

"Any way you want," Arnaud replied, withdrawing his hand shyly. "There's a whole bunch of built-in filters, plus you can download them from the net."

"How you design a filter?"

"Um, here." He invoked the filter design function. "The screen's totally different here. To tell you the truth, I'm not too good at filter design. But the idea is to define the probabilities of note changes over time—so much chance of a whole step, so much for a minor third, like that."

"So you can force one note by setting odds to a hundred?" Julie's hands were already flying over the keyboard. "I get it—this is easy to learn."

Caine walked out onto the porch, eating a piece of boudin. "He force any of his compositions on you?" he asked around a mouthful of food.

"Nah, he just teach me." Julie smiled at Caine. "He a good teacher."

"Yeah, Arnaud's a good boy." Caine smiled back.

"Not like you, you good-for-nothing loafer," Arnaud retorted. "I do all the work around here."

"Yeah, it's hard work snuggling up a to pretty girl, all right."

Julie looked at Caine. "Arnaud here ain't fresh like you. He be a perfect gentleman."

Caine grunted, eyes locked with Julie's. "It's downright unnatural to be a perfect gentleman around a beauty like you."

Julie dropped her eyes to the tone sculptor and busied her hands.

"Come on, Caine," Arnaud said irritably. "Didn't you say that we had work to do?"

"I've been waiting on you, boss," Caine said, grinning. "Ready to roll when you are."

"Ooh, listen!" Julie squealed. The tone sculptor was replicating one of the tunes she'd played the night before. Jeepers Creepers.

"You're a quick study," Arnaud said, clambering into the motorized Corps boat.

"You got more out of my lesson than I did out of your guitar lesson."

"Guitar be a hard instrument. You do okay, learn a couple of chords and how to tune it," she said, tapping furiously at the keyboard while she talked.

"Not as okay as you. Look at you, you're already getting music out of it."

"Oh, I can get music out of most anything," she said. "Marain was right, I do got the gift."

"Yeah, well, we got a job," Caine interjected. "Shake a leg, Svengali."

"I'm coming!" He turned back to Julie. "I'll leave the sculptor with you and pick it up later today, okay?"

"Sure, sure," she said, preoccupied. "See you at supper."

"I guess that qualifies as an invitation," Caine said as they pulled away.

"For me, anyway," Arnaud said.

"That's your problem," Caine replied. "You always wait to be invited. Some things in life you just have to crash."

The tendrils were really thick by now. They kept fouling the pump. There were spots where they'd started solidifying, and the boat had to be portaged. Worst of all were the spots where it was too thick to float through, but too crumbly to portage. It was miserable, sweaty work all day long, but they finally verified that all the residents in their assigned area had been evacuated.

Everyone, that is, except Julie and her aunt.

"We gotta notify Division," Caine said, as they headed toward the LaBas homestead.

"Let's hold off another day," Arnaud said, shoving a gelatinous stalk away from the gunwale with an oar. "We can try to talk sense into them after dinner."

"Be reasonable, Arnaud. I like them too, but they're not going to be able to get out by boat unless they leave tonight. And you know as well as I do that the old lady has no intentions of going anywhere."

"I know," he replied. "But maybe Julie can...."

"Who's thinking with his johnson now? Snap out of it, boy! Nice as they are, those women are trouble. And we gotta report them."

"Look, Caine, I'm the senior officer on the team, and I say we wait."

"Is that an order, sir?"

"Yes."

"Fine, mister." Caine shoved the terminal at Arnaud. "Log it."

Arnaud and Caine were caked with Mud-Dri residue—sticky white streaked with green and orange algae. The old woman eyed them with distaste. "You boys filthy."

"Yes, ma'am," said Arnaud.

"What you been doing out there? Rolling in toothpaste?"

"No, ma'am. Portaging the boat. It's getting mighty thick, ma'am, and it's going to get worse."

"Well, that ain't no reason to be traipsing that crud through my good clean house. Julie!" She shouted, and the young woman appeared at the door.

"Oui, marain?"

"You go get some of your father's clothes for these two." She disappeared back into the cabin.

"Where is her father?" Caine asked, leaning against the porch railing.

"Jesus, Caine! What a tactless jerk you are!"

"That's okay, Arnaud. I don't mind. Her papa got his foot bit off by a gator in '32. The gangrene kill him about a week later."

"I'm sorry," Caine said.

"Ain't your fault. And for your next question: where her mama? After Pierre pass on, she get the craziness and run off to LaPlace—shack up with a drag racer name o' Earl."

"So she's still alive, then?" Arnaud asked.

The old woman spat over the rail. "She dead to me. My own sister, she was, but she abandoned this child and left our home."

Julie came through the screen door with an armful of clothing. "I think they fit you. Be baggy, maybe."

"Thanks. We could use some clean clothes."

"C'mon, Julie," the old woman said. "Let's get inside. You embarrass these boys by watching them undress."

"Okay, marain." As she followed the old woman inside, she tossed a glance over her shoulder at them both. Arnaud blushed, but Caine winked.

After dinner, Arnaud asked Julie, "How'd you do with the tone sculptor?"

"Oh, I get the hang of it pretty quick. You wanna hear what I done?"

"Sure!" he said. She ran into the other room, and returned with the sculptor. She fiddled with the controls, then started the playback.

It was Jeepers Creepers. She'd arranged seven—no, eight tracks. She'd even gotten into the voice filter subsystem and fabricated a trombone. It was uncanny. How could she be so accomplished in one day?

"That's incredible!" Caine said, when the playback stopped. "I've got to send a copy of that to my uncle Gordy."

"Who he?" Julie asked.

"He's sysop at Motown. He's going to flip when he hears you."

Arnaud struggled to keep a sociable smile on his face. He'd begged Caine to send his own sculptures to Caine's uncle, to no avail. Still, Julie's first attempts made his sculptures seem flat and contrived. She really did have the gift. "Listen," Arnaud said, and even to his own ears his voice grated. "We've got to talk about your evacuation."

"We talked about that the day we met," the old woman said.

"You're just being stubborn."

"Don't you get fresh with me," she snapped, "just 'cause my niece play music better than you."

"That has nothing to do with it."

"I'm afraid we do need to discuss it, Miz Lourdes," Caine said. "You've been very kind to us, and we're really fond of you folks. But, whether we like it or not, you've got to move. Tomorrow, maybe next day, that swamp is going to be rock solid. Then the bulldozers come through. They won't stop for you."

"Mmm," she said. "You let me worry about that. This ain't the first time Yankees tried to chase our family out of this swamp."

"But..."

"Quiet, boys." Her voice softened. "You boys been good to me, and I ain't mad at you. But I ain't going, and that is my last word."

"Julie?" Arnaud turned to her. "Can't you talk some sense into your aunt?"

"When she gets like this, there's no turning her," Julie replied. "Besides, this is our land. We got rights, don't we?"

"You'll be compensated by the Relocation Board, but that's it." Caine's voice was blunt. "If you make trouble, you won't even get that."

"Then we won't," the old woman said. "You ready for some bread pudding and whiskey sauce?"

As Caine set up the campsite, Arnaud sent a frantic e-mail to the divisional commander, Colonel Wolfgang, explaining the situation and asking for an extension. The colonel curtly declined, directing Arnaud to lead the involuntary relocation task force, which would rendezvous with him at 0700, while he, the colonel, observed and evaluated Arnaud's command qualifications.

Usually the Corps was pretty informal, Arnaud brooded as he cleared the screen. When they went all military on you, you were in it—but deep.

For a change, Caine wasn't talking his ear off. That suited Arnaud fine. It left him free to toss and turn in his sleeping bag.

He must've fallen asleep, because his alarm woke him as it went off. 0600. His mouth felt like it had been glued shut with library paste.

Caine was nowhere in sight. He'd broken camp early; all his gear was gone. Arnaud supposed he was back at the LaBas shack, in a last-minute attempt to talk some sense into that stubborn old woman. The swamp had thickened so much overnight that the boat was now useless. Arnaud began hiking toward Julie's house. He ran into the task force en route.

"Where's the colonel?" he asked the squad leader as he read the man's name badge. Corporal Ryzscowski.

"He's at the perimeter, sir."

"Perimeter?"

"Yes, sir. Apparently one of the residents fired a weapon at our reconnaissance team."

"Anyone hurt?"

"Private Jenkins was hit, sir, but she's doing all right. It was just rock salt. Stung pretty bad, though."

"Yeah, that sounds like the old woman."

By now they were within sight of the house. The colonel stalked up to Arnaud. "This woman is a menace, lieutenant."

"So I'm told, sir." Arnaud shifted uneasily under the colonel's glare as the corporal snickered.

"What kind of terms are you on with this woman?" the colonel asked. "She keeps asking for you."

"Uh, pretty friendly, I guess, sir. Caine and I have had a number of discussions with her. Where is he, anyway?"

"How would I know? He was under your command."

"He's probably inside, then. May I approach the house?"

"Do as you see fit, Lieutenant. I'm just observing here. Just try not to get killed."

Arnaud walked about halfway to the house, then stopped. "Miz Lourdes! Can you hear me? It's Arnaud Bechet!" He pronounced it Cajun-style.

"No call to yell, boy. I ain't deaf." He could see her through the screen door. "So you finally learned your own name, eh?"

"Yes ma'am. Can I come in?"

"Yeah, you best."

He walked up to the porch, then through the screen door. The old woman sat in her rocking chair, shotgun in her lap. There was a hole in the screen door that hadn't been there before.

"You all right, Miz Lourdes?" he asked.

"Mad enough to chew nails, but I ain't been shot or nothing."

"Well, that's a relief." He looked around the house. "Where's Julie? Isn't Caine here with you?"

"Why you think I'm so mad? Them two run off last night."

"What!"

"Sure. He call his uncle on that computer, and uncle likes Julie's music. So they off to Detroit together. Cleared out of here round midnight." The old woman's knuckles whitened around the shotgun. "She ain't no better than her mama. He say he gonna be her agent. Agent my ass. Oh, they done stole your music box, too."

Arnaud sat down, stunned. Julie was gone?

The old woman patted him on his knee. "I know you be smitten by her, but take it like a man."

"Oh, I wasn't in love with her!" he denied. "I'm just...surprised, that's all."

"You can't lie any better than that Yankee partner of yours. But I don't mind." She reached down beside the rocking chair. "You take this guitar, boy. That's only fair, since she took your music box."

Arnaud took the handle of the guitar case without thinking. He didn't love Julie. Did he?

"You better go now, Arnaud. There be trouble here, and I don't want you mixed up in it." She patted his knee again. "You a good boy."

Arnaud tried to shake off his daze. "You'd better give me the shotgun, Miz Lourdes."

"You know I ain't gonna."

"They'll take you to jail if you don't," he said earnestly. "They're not playing around."

"You think I be playing? Take me out of this swamp, and anywhere be a jail for me. I could never live in some damn Yankee suburb." She sniffed back a tear. "Specially without my little Julie. You run along now, cher."

"But..."

She pointed the gun at his head. "I said, run along, cher. Miz Lourdes too busy for company today."

He gulped. "Yes ma'am." Then he turned his back and walked through that screen door once more. He walked across the crumbling, milky yard, past the colonel, toward camp.

The colonel chased him. "What's going on here, mister? Stop right there and explain yourself."

"I quit." Arnaud didn't even break stride. "You'll have to kill that old lady without my help."

The colonel sputtered for a minute, then turned back to assume command of the task force. Arnaud heard the grenade launcher fire a couple of times. Those would be tear gas canisters, he guessed. He didn't have to guess about the shotgun blasts.

When he got back to the campsite, he sat down. The whole swamp had turned to chalk. Arid and brittle. Like his heart. He opened the case, then pulled out the guitar and started tuning up. It was hard on the nerves. The closer he got, the worse it sounded.   *-dp-*

CHASING THE BIRDS

by Patricia Russo

The night was chilly, and he'd left his jacket behind, afraid the click of the closet door would wake his mother. He slapped his arms, making the bags of seeds and bread crusts rattle like maracas. That was okay, though. She couldn't hear him now. He was totally alone, the only person up and about for miles. He liked that; it gave him a charge, got his blood zinging. A man of mystery on a mission. Right. Who had to sneak out of his house like some pissant kid. It made him sick. But he wouldn't let Momma's bitchiness ruin his good mood, no sir.

He paused at the top of the hill, panting, his breath pale vapor trails in the predawn darkness. Another quarter mile to the lake, but all downhill now. I'm out of shape, he thought. Her fault, always keeping him inside doing dumb chores, sorting the buttons she'd collected in cookie tins over decades, for chrissakes. As soon as he finished with one thing, she thought up ten more stupid jobs for him to do. You're not paying rent, so make yourself useful, she said. Shit. And those huge meals she cooked. What killed him was the broken hearted expression she pasted on her face if he said he'd like cereal instead of steak and eggs and hash browns and cinnamon buns for breakfast, or a simple sandwich instead of a seven-course dinner. Of course he had to eat it then, whatever she'd cooked. Hamburgers dripping with grease, that horrible rice pudding with heavy cream. The one time he didn't, she'd actually cried.

Jesus, he was still puffing. He must've gained forty pounds since he moved back in with her. Fifty, maybe. He was forty-seven. His dad had stroked out at fifty. He had better take care of himself.

Starting down the hill, watching his feet, he vowed to work out more. Set up some weights in the basement, maybe. Get himself a treadmill or one of those climbing-stairs machines. He was edging into heart-attack country.

Plus, last time he'd sneaked down to the lake, all the big silver birds had gotten away. Used to be he could catch one easily. Two, on a good night. But last time, all he'd grabbed was air. Ended up doing a belly flop in the grass and taking a knock on the chin that made his teeth rattle. And the birds exploded into the sky, the backwash from their enormous wings battering him breathless, stretched out on the ground clutching two handfuls of nothing. Yeah, he'd been out of practice, but it was humiliating. They were awkward on land, those birds. Slow and top-heavy, mincing along on reed-thin legs. They needed a good twenty-foot run to build the momentum to take to the air. Because of their huge wingspan, he figured. Colossal wingspan. Once they got airborne, they flew fast. Good swimmers, too. On land, though, they were handicapped. Knock them down, flip them over, a knee on the breast bone, finished. Easy.

Or it used to be. Trudging down the path, he thought again how great it'd be if she let him have a gun. But no. Momma'd rather chew glass than have a gun in the house. No pistol, no rifle, no shotgun. Over her dead body, she said, and he'd considered that for a minute or two, until he remembered the social security checks would stop.

Bossy bitch.

He heard the water now, the lake lapping softly at the shore. The sky was growing lighter. He didn't have much time. The birds stopped at the lake only briefly, just before dawn. Where they came from and where they went, he didn't know, except that they flew in from the east and flew off to the west. As soon as the top edge of the sun broke over the horizon, the flock lifted off, vanishing within seconds.

The breeze picked up, gusting across the lake and making the reeds on the bank whisper and quake. The wind felt clammy; he shivered as he left the path and cut across the sedgy ground.

It'd been so long since he'd been to the lake, he was afraid that the spot, his spot—the bare, stony patch of ground a few yards from the water's edge where he spread his hoarded bread crusts and the seeds he secretly harvested from Momma's garden—had changed. Or simply disappeared. Stranger things had happened than a piece of ground altering form. But it was there, bare and perfect as ever. Grinning, he ripped open the bags and scattered the seeds, strewed handfuls of hard crusts.

You'd think they'd avoid this place after being caught here so often. But the big silver birds were as dumb as dirt. Bird-brained. He giggled. Time was, he'd trek down here every night. The birds always returned, despite his predations.

Always fell for the seeds and bread, too.

He figured there was good reason for that. The birds must be on the wing all night, or damn near. They broke their journey at the lake, last rest-stop before morning. And they had to be starving. Hell, he'd be starving too if he'd done that much flying. And hey, guess what—free food. Of course they fell for it, dumb-ass bird-brained birds.

Wadding up the bags, he glanced at the sky. Half an hour until sunrise, maybe less. If their routine hadn't changed, the flock should be descending on the lake within minutes.

He shoved the bags in his pocket and rubbed his arms again. Man, he had goosepimples. It'd been way too long. He really missed it. And now he was going to get it.

Parting the reeds, careful not to break even one, he crept into cover. The ground was damp; the knees of his jeans soaked through immediately. He didn't care. Holding his breath, he listened for the flock's approach. He heard it: the slow, percussive sound of enormous wings flapping, distant still but coming nearer with each passing second.

From within the reeds, he watched the birds descend.

Twelve of them, their silvery feathers aglow even in the gray predawn light. A wingspan longer than his body, and sinuous necks, like swans. But they weren't swans; that he was sure of. Their bodies were too big, their legs too long, their beaks were the wrong shape, too wide, too blunt. A couple of times he'd paged through bird books, looking for them, but wasn't surprised that no illustration came close. They weren't truly birds, after all, so why should their bird shapes be that of real birds?

The flock alighted on the lake, dropping silently from the sky, making no sound as they touched the water. Folding their wings, the twelve silver creatures swam to shore.

He hugged himself. The birds stepped out of the water like graceful stilt-dancers, their movements in sync, left, right, bob-your-head, twelve identical steps each. He could smell their wet feathers. Half of him hoped they would shed their skins. The other half preferred them like this, wild, avian, soft as down pillows.

He'd had them both ways.

He rose to a crouch and tensed, steeling himself. The birds were oblivious to him, ignoring the trembling of the weeds as he shifted position. Dumb as shit as birds, they were, and not much brighter when they weren't.

Excited now, he fought to hold himself back, to wait for the exact, perfect moment. His nerve-endings were on fire, the blood hummed in his ears, a sound that made him think of hornets.

He had to be fast, fast as a hornet. He took a deep breath, readying himself.

The birds spotted the food and daintily, in delicate lock-step, minced toward the crusts and carefully scattered seeds, passing his hiding place without turning their heads.

He waited until they had their backs to him; about to burst, he waited one more dizzying moment until each had bent a long, swan-like neck to the ground. Then he jumped from the reeds.

And his mother charged down the hill, screaming at the top of her voice, waving a broom over her head like a demented hag out of a nightmare. The birds scattered, their lock-step choreography shattered by terror, running in all directions and flinging themselves up, out of his grasp, out of human reach, vanishing into the sky.

He gaped at her. She'd run out of the house in her nightgown and an old pair of rubber boots, her hair a wild white mare's nest, her teeth still in the bathroom medicine cabinet. A fat old woman, leaning on a broom, gasping for air.

He burst into tears. He sank to the ground and sobbed.

"Get up," she hissed. "Get up and come home now."

"Bitch," he moaned, rocking. "Bitch, bitch, bitch."

She got him home. Cooked him breakfast. She sipped tea while he ate, just to be doing something. She could not bear to look at him, her son, her only child.

She'd thought...she let herself hope it was over. Finished. It'd been months since he last sneaked out of the house at night, and then, though she hadn't woken in time to follow him, she was fairly sure nothing had happened. She'd found no blood, no feathers, no...signs of a struggle. She'd let herself be relieved. She'd persuaded herself that he'd only gone down there to look.

That all he cared to do now was look at the birds.

It was possible.

She still thought it was possible. She believed, fiercely, that people could change. After he'd eaten, she made him scrub the kitchen floor and then set him to stripping the wallpaper in the spare room, though it didn't need replacing. Tire him out, she told herself as she fixed a big lunch. Wear him out and feed him up and all he'll want to do tonight is sleep.

She wished he'd never come home.

The day he'd come up the gravel walk with his belongings in an old gym bag and one paper grocery sack, pushed right in, sat down at the table like he had a right to be there, her man had been dead twenty years. Her man. This boy's father. Last time she'd set eyes on the boy'd been one week to the day after the funeral. He'd left home with more luggage than he came back with. Took the pickup, took his father's cigar box of buffalo-head nickels, took Grandma's ring, took the bankbook. Seventeen then. Thirty-seven when he came back.

Forty-seven now. Still her boy. Her only child.

She thanked God his father had died without ever knowing.

She wished she'd never seen what he did down at the lake.

It made her wonder what he might have got up to those years he was on his own. Imagining such things made her want to cry. Scream. Stick her head in the oven—but suicide was wrong, and she'd never held with it. It scared her that she thought about suicide so much; it scared her even more that it might be the only way to get those thoughts, those pictures, out of her mind.

No. She'd never been a coward. Spitting distance from eighty, she wasn't going to turn one now.

She'd never been weak, either. Always reckoned herself a strong person. Farm life wasn't for weaklings. Neither was getting old. Had to have grit and muscle for both. She'd always judged she had plenty. Until her son came home.

She couldn't lock him in his room. He was a grown man. He could knock the door off its hinges with one good kick.

He clumped into the kitchen and sat down to lunch, scowling. She ladled gravy over a plateful of biscuits, piled another plate high with pan-fried chicken. She poured him buttermilk to drink, and iced tea with plenty of sugar. He muttered something that might have been thanks but was more likely a curse. Her hearing wasn't so good anymore. She never imagined she'd be glad of that.

That night, she stayed awake, sitting up in the straight-backed chair, drinking coffee despite how bad it was for her blood pressure, listening. Though the nights got cold, she kept her bedroom window open, so if she missed hearing him on the stairs, she'd catch the crunch of his footsteps on the gravel walk. But nothing happened. A week passed, then two, and once more she began to hope it might really be finished. People could change. She'd believed that all her life.

Hoping, she slept again, as much as a woman close to eighty could sleep. In the paper she read you needed less sleep when you got older, but that wasn't true. You needed as much as ever, you just couldn't get it. Sleep was now a fragile thread, breakable by the least whisper, the slightest twitch.

She woke with her heart pounding. The glowing numbers of her clock radio read 5:37. She came out of blackness into gray half-light so abruptly it dizzied her. She pressed her hand to her breastbone, thinking: a dream, just a dream I don't remember.

But when she got up and checked his room, he was gone.

She clenched her fists, biting back tears. Too late, too late. He had too big a start on her. Even now, the birds must be circling the lake, coming in to land on the water.

Her heart raced; every breath went through her like a knife. She pulled on her old boots, threw a sweater over her shoulders, and ran.

People can change, she told herself as she pounded up the path. She'd worked all her life, hard work, farm work. Her bones were strong, but they were still nearly eighty years old, and each step shot slivers of white-hot pain into knee and ankle, hip and spine. People could will themselves to change, could turn their lives around. People could surprise you. They could even make you proud.

She crested the hill as the sun edged over the horizon. By the time she reached the lake, the sky was streaked with pink. Red sky at morning. That was bad, wasn't it? she thought. That was bad.

Worse was seeing her son atop the strangled bird, his pants around his knees, his hairy white buttocks pumping. The bird's great wings had relaxed in death; half bent, they hid him from view as he thrust a last time, then collapsed on the body. She stared at the bird's neck, the neat silver feathers mottled with blood.

She'd guessed, but this was the first time she'd seen it. Once before she'd caught him, but then he'd waited until the creatures had taken off their birdskins and assumed their other form. He'd raped two but had done no murder then. Seeing the creatures snatch up their skins and dress themselves in bird-shape, then leap, enormous and silver-winged, into the sky, for an instant had blotted out the image of flailing, featherless limbs and pale necks straining to scream but making no sound. They had no voices, these beings, neither as women nor as birds. For a moment only, a split second, she had felt pure awe.

The awe died, swamped by shock.

Grief.

Horror.

It should have killed her, seeing that. But she had lived.

And this, now, was even worse. She'd guessed, from the feathers—and the blood— but knowing for sure was a thousand times more terrible.

This was her son, her only child.

She could hear his breaths, ragged from exertion, smooth and lengthen into the rhythm of sleep. Sick, heartbroken, she listened to his breaths become snuffles and then snores and thought: he'll catch cold, lying here, the ground's so damp....

Then in a rush she thought: I could kill him now. Her heart fluttered, and she almost cried out. Dizzy, she sat down on the wet ground and squeezed her head between her hands. The thought was jolting, so unexpected and dreadful it left her gasping, but at the same time it felt old, a secret that had hidden in her mind for years, waiting to be rediscovered. He wouldn't stop, or couldn't stop, but she could stop him.

As a child, cutting up bad, sassing, she remembered her mother snapping: I brought you into this world, and I can take you right out of it. But the worst Ma ever did was switch her bare legs with a peach-tree twig. I could kill him, she thought, and her heart raced wildly.

She got to her feet. Quick, now, before he wakes. You have to do it now.

Just off the path, at the bottom of the hill, lay a scattering of stones, kicked there by hikers or washed down by rain. One was near the size of the footstool she used to reach the top shelf of her pantry, and rough-ly the same shape—rectangular, maybe a foot and a half long and half that across. Lift with your legs, not your back, her daddy had taught her, so she squatted to pick it up. Her muscles groaned, and she felt something pop between her shoulder blades. Heavy, jesus it was heavy, she couldn't carry it the three, four yards to where her son lay, it was impossible.

She carried it, sweat running cold all over her body. She stood over him, panting, every nerve screaming. Lift it, she thought. Hoist it up as high as you can, then let it go.

Or just let go. It's heavy enough.

She centered the stone over her son's head; she stared at the rest of him, his back rising and falling, his bare buttocks goosebumped from the chill air, his jeans bagged around his knees, the worn soles of his running shoes.

Drop it, she ordered herself, but even as she formed the words in her mind she was turning, swinging the stone away from his head, releasing it to thump on the damp ground. The rock scraped her hands; beads of blood welled up on her palms. She closed her fists, welcoming the pain. Her son did not stir. He snored softly, his breath ruffling the silver-white feathers on the dead bird's breast.

He woke with a start. The sun beat down on the back of his neck. And other places. Scrambling to his feet, he hiked up his trousers, buttoned and zipped. Shit, he thought. I fell asleep. Grabbing the dead bird by the feet, he dragged it to the edge of the lake and, grunting, heaved it in. Then he returned to the spot, his special spot, and kicked dirt over a few pinfeathers and droplets of blood.

Puzzled, he stared a moment at a thick, flattish rock. It hadn't been there before.

Maybe he simply hadn't noticed, in the dark? Stooping, he peered closer and spotted traces of blood on the rough gray stone. Okay, he just hadn't seen it. He spat on the rock and scrubbed it with his sleeve, rubbing the blood away.

She sat up that night, in the straight-backed chair, with the window open, sipping black coffee, the boots next to the chair, a sweater on her lap.

She sat up every night, in the straight-backed chair, with the window wide open, her boots beside her and her sweater folded neatly on her lap.

And, with tears in her eyes, planned menus.

-dp-

PANSPERMIA

drifting between the stars
many thousands of years,
its smashed chromosomes
defying a million-plus
rads of ionizing radiation
by bridging base pair fragments
Deinococcus accretes
shell of interstellar
crud that shields its
scorching entry through
planetary atmosphere to
a gentler place
to grow

—**John Benson and Tina Reigel**

DANSE MACABRE

During the days of devastation
missiles of madness were launched.
Arsenals were emptied and there
was no end to mass annihilation.
Vain regrets stalked our reveries
and fractured our tortured dreams.

Before the birth of bedlam
the rad count found new heights
Numbers were processed
at faster-than-light speeds.
We plumbed the pages of history,
fashioning new manifestoes from old.

By the terms of the tragedy
clouds gathered like dreadnoughts
for the storms of a pandemic winter.
Mountains of ice scoured the plains
and forests to a pitted moraine.
Forests of nightmare infested our brains.

After the coronation of chaos
the seas boiled and whales burned,
their dread cadavers riding the tides
to clog our beaches and harbors,
to scatter the blackened horizon
like the hulls of broken galleons.

With the ascent of anarchy
states and sovereignties dissolved.
We watched the cities gravel into ruin,
skytowers capsized in a shifting jigsaw mass,
great bridges wrenched from their sockets,
reduced to an anguish of metal ligaments.

In the postmortem of pandemonium
the dreams of an entire generation
were ground to fodder and reprocessed
to feed the maw of an uncertain future.
All our conceptions were slaughtered
and rendered and spent as the past.

During the days of devastation,
before the birth of bedlam,
by the terms of the tragedy,
after the coronation of chaos,
with the ascent of anarchy,
in the postmortem of pandemonium,

the nightmare of history continued
to unravel at a breakneck pace.
Moralities and principles were gutted
for the greater needs of the moment.
We clung to an existence we could
never before have imagined.

The veins in our arms protrude
as we settle into the bones of
whatever it is we have become.
The fount of human memory fades
as the gibberish of our lives
claims our times and minds.

Somewhere in the distance an idiot
is beating on a tin pot with a spoon
and another idiot or two joins in.
Though there is no shred of melody
and the rhythms keep changing,
we have all begun a crazy dance.

—Bruce Boston

THE TOWER

by M. L. Ching

Three days from Babel, over the crest of a dune, we caught our first glimpse of the Tower.

Since early morning, the caravan had slunk through the open desert waste at a sedate pace, savoring the oppressive flavor of the sand barrens in the manner of ascetics luxuriating in the sting of the whips they clap across their own backs. Michael and I, masquerading as a wealthy Alexandrian merchant and his servant, rode at an honored place near the front of the procession, within shouting distance of the caravan leader, a stocky nomad whose terrible visage—a leathery landscape eroded by the desert wind and irrigated by the scars of a hundred battles with desert raiders—freely broke into a jovial grin despite his bleak surroundings. Whenever the demands of his position allowed, which was often enough, he fell back beside us and told us his stories: bandits beaten, ambushes avoided, blockades circumvented, times of near starvation while carting untold amounts of wealth from one oasis to the next. The repetitive boredom of travel on the camel trains wears on the mind; ridge after ridge of wind-blown sand makes wild even the most domesticated countenances, visions horrifying and beautiful lurk in the peripheries, and the wind itself recalls voices one thought had been forever silenced. "Horrrerrr, horrrerrr," they moan through the wagons and over the dead sand. It all left me eager for the innumerable tales of this Bedouin troll. "Never once," he claimed, "in twenty years upon this sea have I lost a caravan. A few men, some camels, a finger, but the caravans have always survived the voyage." He held up his left hand for our inspection. The smallest digit ended in the middle of the first bone. I nodded appreciatively. Michael gave it a derisive glance and turned his gaze back to the distant horizon ahead.

Michael had spent the previous weeks of the journey fuming with impatience. He set himself firmly against every detail of the trip. He considered himself above the method of travel itself and saw no reason to move in this manner. He called the camels "unpleasant, foul-tempered beasts who should be glad to have any rider at all, taking into account their pungency" and thought even less of the Bedouin guards and merchants for their "naïve beliefs and foolish traditions, hardly more than apes." Constantly I had to admonish him of our need for an inconspicuous entrance into the city. Otherwise, I am sure he would have simply abandoned the caravan and flown there directly, landing in a flourish of trumpets. As it was, he rode in a passive, black mood the whole way, for which I concocted a variety of excuses so as not to offend our companions.

It was out of this mood that he rose that day. He turned to face me and pointed at the horizon, his voice triumphantly resonating as he declared, "Behold, Gabriel, our destination is within sight."

I scanned the desert skeptically. Babel lay about twenty-three leagues distant and would not be in sight for another two days. At first I saw nothing, and I began to tell him that he was mistaken, but then I spotted a thin, dark needle rising from the far wastes, too distant to discern any details, but unquestionably there. Michael had not pointed out the city, but our true destination, the Tower of Babel.

"Oh yes, you see the Tower," the caravan leader piped happily. "Many ports have I sailed to in my twenty years on this sea, and nowhere have I witnessed a wonder as wondrous."

"It must stand nigh a mile high to allow us a view from here," I murmured.

"Oh, no, my friend. It is much, much taller than that. And they say that when it is finished," he added, a note of awe softening his jovial tone almost to a whisper, "it will reach to the Heavens themselves."

I glanced at Michael. No longer edgy, he gazed thoughtfully at the Tower. But his fingers, long and delicate, dug into his saddle so tensely that I felt they would snap from the pressure.

When He recruited us, His Heavenly Host, His Holy Army of spirits, we the proud and distant seraphim, the aristocratic cherubim, the bureaucracy of arch-angels, the rank-and-file of the common angel, it became quickly obvious that some subtle forms of self-deception would be necessary to stand as a servant of Jehovah. None of those who were faithful to the end could be counted innocent of self-delusion. If we had actually dissected the nature of his commandments, some of them cruel beyond reason, our better natures would have rebelled. We relieved ourselves of this responsibility with clever usage of the adjective "inscrutable." We did not serve because of our faith. We *invented* faith in order to serve. The nature of the loyalty He demanded of us required nothing less.

The Fallen Ones were the notable exceptions, Lucifer the most notable among them. He continually badgered our Lord for motives and reasons, asked about long-term effects and plans, and denied His basic ineffability, which the rest of us had "wisely" accepted. Jehovah waved all these aside with a stockpile of amused and cryptic phrases. After several millennia of constant interrogation frustrated by Jehovah, Lucifer, called the Morningstar, broke. "In the end," he said at our last meeting before the War in Heaven, "our reckoning will come not for what we have won or lost, but how we faced triumph or defeat." His blue eyes and languid, paling seraph's face shone cryptic in the light of his candle. "Our Lord says fight for Him, serve in His name, and you do good. That's the only way to gain His Grace. His rewards are only for those who obey Him. I say fight for yourself, in your own name, and gain the only love you really deserve, the only love that can truly be perfect: your own." He hesitated, studying me as I studied him. I could not be sure what he saw. I found his expression to be worn and sickly. *Such is the fate of those who would defy Him*, I thought. He continued. "Very soon, Gabriel, I will go to war. Michael will lead Our Lord's host against me and my companions, and we will lose. Many of our friends will die, on both sides. You will fight at Michael's side, and you'll help to cast me down. You'll listen silently as others denounce me as Deceiver and the Prince of Lies. You'll accept all this." I protested to the contrary, and he cut me off. "You will accept this because I'm telling you now that when I go back to the whirls of power from whence we came, I'll claim rightfully that I am clean, that I know myself....It is not through God's Grace that a seed becomes a tree." He stood to his fullest height, and I no longer perceived a sickness. The stark marble walls of my chamber reflected and intensified his light. "So long, Gabriel. When we meet again, we will battle, but you are always a friend." Then he was gone.

The general mood of the caravan lifted with the sighting of the Tower, and this new exuberance carried over through the next two days. As the far-off edifice loomed before us, the merchants harassed each other and made bets on the amounts of their goods that they would sell on their arrival.

The Bedouin guards, comfortable that no bandits roamed this close to the city, drifted from the side of the procession, relaxed and lighthearted, racing during the day, hunting the scavenger birds with their bows at night. The servants, after tying down and feeding the camels and stock animals, drank spirits brewed from dates and gambled with the marked bones of cats, smuggled out of Egypt, where felines had recently been declared sacred animals. The troll and I rode together mostly, and he entertained me while I responded as expected of the servant of a wealthy Egyptian. I stole his hunting knife and provided him with the opportunity to pilfer an extra traveling cloak, which he took. We wore them conspicuously, laughed the matter to death, and in this way became great friends.

Michael, alone in the caravan, held on to the empty, windswept attitude of the desert. Sour faced and disgusted, his glance drained the buoyancy from any man's mood, and the travelers all avoided it as well as they could. He followed me along, the shadow of my mission, the constant reminder that hung over me and voided my simple, evasive pleasures.

The Tower drew nearer, and at noon, a day away, we could distinguish the mural which wrapped around it, spiraling organically from the horizon, where a man knelt unharmed between the jaws of a lion five times his size and painted its teeth, one by one. Each tooth depicted a different figure, men and women of an insatiable beauty. Gods, I assumed, of the city's pantheon. After the artist finished them, each sprang from the maw of the great beast and hurled itself into the spiral. Just above the lion, the mural showed a harsh, unsympathetic waste, a deadly and desolate land, but each time the spiral swung from the side of the Tower to meet our gaze, the Gods instilled small changes along their journey, which I realized was not one through space but through eons. Upon this edifice, the citizens of Babel wrote the Creation. I followed the spiral up, observing the Gods as they sowed the land with rain, created the moon to ease the sun's abuse, and littered the world with plants and animals. Then, near the height where I could no longer perceive what the mural depicted, lay the lion in the Paradise shaped by the Gods. And out of the lion's mouth crept man and woman.

This story riddled me. I asked my guide what it meant.

"I have sailed upon this sea for twenty years, and I have heard many tellings of how the world came to be as it is today. None have ever suited me as true, but this one pleases me the most. At the bottom, which you will not see until we reach the city tomorrow," he said, pointing at the Tower as if this simple gesture would reveal the hidden portions, "it shows the beginning, with nothing but mankind suffering in a savage world with no life. So unrelenting was the heat of the sun and scarcity of food that the people made a deal with a giant lion. They would live in his throat and he would hunt for them all. In exchange, if there were no animals to hunt on a day, one man or woman would travel down his throat to his stomach to be consumed. But it was not long before the lion tried to trick them. He would roam around listlessly with his mouth closed so no one could see outside and claim the land was empty of things to hunt. This way the lion would be fed without any effort while the people went hungry. They asked the lion to try harder, but he said they were free to leave at any time, although that meant a certain death for them. They devised a plan.

"One day a man called out to the lion, 'Dear friend, lion. We are so grateful to you for our refuge, we wish to present a gift to you.'

"'Ha, ha,' the lion chuckled, 'you have been giving me all the gifts I need. Never have I been so well fed before now.'

"'Yes, but that was only our side of the bargain,' the man replied, 'this is our gift to you. I wish to paint your teeth, so when you meet the giant lioness, you need only to smile and she will be unable to resist you.'

"The lion, whose pride was no match for his vanity, was intrigued. 'If you truly can do this, then make it so.'

"The man went to work and painted upon the teeth of the lion the ones who would create in the world what the people needed: Rain, fertile lands, the night with its mother the moon, clouds, all the plants and creatures, lakes and rivers. Thirty-two Creators in all. When he finished, the thirty-two Creators wrested the teeth from the lion's jaws and formed their bodies from them. Then they worked their ways upon the world.

"The lion was so angered by this trickery that he threatened to bury his head in the sand until both he and the people suffocated. But before he could even dig a hole, a rabbit hopped right up to his face and practically begged to be caught. And many more leapt through the land. Such bounty as he had never seen. The people lived well inside the lion's throat from then until the world was ready for them. Afterwards, the Gods became exhausted from their efforts, and fell to sleep. The lion took them up and replaced them in his jaws. They remain to this day as figures painted upon its teeth, sleeping until the time comes when they are needed once more."

"But if these gods that remade the world were in fact created by man, where did man come from?" I asked.

The little troll laughed and shook his head, as if he had just been told tea leaves had attacked his mother. "Yes, that is the hole, is it not? Who created these beings that suffered and remade the world? The old man who gave to me the story as I have told it to you, I asked him just that question. How did he answer me? 'What makes you to think man has yet been created?' he says. Then he walks away. Strange, is it not? Just more nonsense, it seems, for a pile of nonsense." He trotted his horse off to the head of the caravan, leaving us in our own thoughts.

I read the story of the Tower over again in my eyes. Its dimensions pulled at me. It yanked at my heart lovingly. I felt like a vessel being towed to safe harbor. I wanted to rest at the base of it, a foundation where men existed but had never been made.

Michael broke the spell. "Vanity," he snarled. "They take pride in their 'achievements' and it brings them low. Very soon they will learn true Glory, through the Grace of Our Lord, so that they may be lifted." A cruel smile curled his lips.

"May Our Lord grant that I never fall in need of such favors," I muttered.

I am tempted, for many reasons, to turn an unsympathetic eye to Michael. Callous, commanding, his piety drained him of the ability for compassion. Incredibly intuitive to the motivations of others but blind to his own, he was the mold by which zealots were cast. When given the place at the Lord's right hand, he struck his own burgeoning ideas from his mind so he could more easily gather opinions from His commands. "Yahweh's lapdog," the cherubim called him from behind cupped hands with a wink and a chuckle, and mostly their comments rang true. Michael could not have been his own being if he had tried. Of all the angels in His command, Michael was the only one He created Himself, and he was a faulty archetype, a failed attempt. Graceful, yes, in both senses of the word. Beautifully formed with all the trappings of motion and balance, he was shortsighted, unoriginal, contemptuous or even wholly unaware of everything Jehovah had not specifically ordained as Beauty. I found it all too easy to judge him harshly.

However, now that it no longer matters how I regard him, I am left with no choice but to pity him. A breach in view drove us apart early on, and by the time I understood him, I could not traverse it by any means. The shame of Michael is that he could never have chosen anything other than he was. When He formed him, Our Lord took the time to grant him free will, to be sure, but never gave him any reason to utilize it. Michael's mind was a sharp analytical knife which, I am certain, would have eventually cut to the truth—had he only been given a doubt, a cause to search truth out. But Jehovah coddled him from the start and spoiled his objectivity. This neglect in Michael's education, I discovered later, spurred Lucifer to his revolt. "Although he has never known me, Michael despises me," Lucifer would say to me eons afterward, his eyes glowing vehemently, casting dark shadows upon his lantern, "and the essence of that hate drove the cleft between myself and your Lord, who had been to each other as two sides of a mountain."

I cannot allow myself the same excuses. Revile me more than my companion, for although I had the misgivings, the opportunities, and the cause to choose a different path, I ignored them all. I buried them when I buried Babel, when I buried Sodom and Gomorrah, when I buried men and women for no more than the whim of my master. I had neither the spiritual courage to maintain my faith in the weight of injustice, as Rafael did, nor the decisive belief in my own conceptions of good and evil, no matter how inexperienced, as Lucifer had. I simply obeyed. One of the many trained lackeys of Heaven. Milton would hallucinate us as a choir, where truly nothing stood but a bureaucracy.

Thus it was that we two avenging angels, carried on the desert's breath, stood upon a dune and surveyed the city of Babel for the first time. Some members of the caravan, who had visited this place before, cried with delight. For those of us who arrived new—expecting yet another busy, putrid trade center, bustling with thieves and littered with haphazardly constructed thatch and mud buildings, plagued with the listless oppression of the hot sands—we could only stand agape. In the midst of leagues of sandy barren, the site of the town was an impossibly green valley dotted with farms and clumps of palms. A lush grassland extended from the city to the top of the valley on all sides and stopped short, holding back the desert forcefully, preventing it from encroaching on the lives of the inhabitants.

And in the center of the valley, the Tower erupting from its southern edge like a roofbeam to hold up the sky, lay the city itself, for which I have still not found any comparisons. Not another random, slipshod arrangement of structures, this metropolis, but a metal masterpiece, low to the ground, organically shaped. No jerrybuilt potteries scrunched between the splendid government buildings on one side and the gaudy cat houses on the other. The edifices of Babel were designed to appear as if they had grown from each other. The houses gave birth to conical causeways that arced over the streets and intersected with others. All

edges and corners had been rounded off. To my eyes, it appeared more a colony of living cells, an organism, than a city. "It is a thing alive, this place," I whispered, awed.

Beside me, Michael was also affected by the sight of Babel, although in a much different manner. "Yes, it is alive," he said, "much in the way that a boil or a blister lives. It is time, I think, for this one to be lanced."

I dried up inside.

We passed through the gates of the city. The Babelites made way for the caravan to enter and greeted us warmly. I pulled my hood up over my eyes so I would not have to meet theirs.

We arrived in the midst of a celebration. Everywhere we heard cheers and raucous yells. A jubilant mood prevailed throughout the populace. Fire dancers crossed our path every few yards, swinging their chains dangerously close to us. On both sides there stood a variety of performers, troubadours, sword swallowers, illusionists, eastern yogis with sharp nails digging into one cheek and emerging from the other, dancers from the northern tribes of Africa, and stranger sights yet. Men sped by on wheels tied to their feet, and others flew through the air above. And through it all, aside from the happy exclamations, the people seemed not to speak much. Even vendors, I noticed, could tell which of the hundreds of inhabitants on the street would approach his stall next, and he would have their goods prepared for them when they arrived, so that many transactions occurred wordlessly. Their method of communication remains a mystery to me still, having been derived mainly, I assume, from a complex system of body gestures and eye movements. Babel's real accomplishment was not the Tower, or the city itself, or even the technology which built them, but the spring from which all these flowed—its people, in their peaceful strangeness, in their graceful, effortless movements, in their diversity of spirit that would not exist so serenely ever again.

A round-eyed serving boy from the caravan, upon seeing the continual sense of innocent play, asked my friend the troll, "What festival is this?"

The old Bedouin laughed. "Twenty years in all seasons I have sailed the sea to this port, and every time, this is what I have seen. This is no festival, my boy. In the city of Babel, this is life."

And I was there to end it.

Early on, Lucifer told me it would end.

Mortals count themselves blessed if they grasp infinity within their lifetimes. They find reason to rejoice in the timeless pull of atoms and gods so long as their place in it is assured. At any given time, there are only a handful of humans alive who understand this.

Lucifer stood alone among the host of paradoxically shortsighted immortals as the only one with a sense of the finite. He alone realized that all things, even that which is endless, must at some time, through some hand or none, come to an end, and that they become no less eternal for doing so.

At night, light refracted from the four corners of time cast a spectrum of hues through the city of Babel. Fox-carts and roller-bladers skittered through the purple-red-green-yellow-blue streets, past the fortunetellers with nothing but happy prophecies. Packs of lions padded past, minded only by the lamb assigned to herd them. In that place in the dark, the fantastical played

poker with the chimerical. A team of Muses danced gaily to a melody piped by an unlikely virgin raised by satyrs, while sprites plucked out the harmony upon a spider web, and a poet in an ascot and a morning coat sat wide-eyed and drunk, composing the verses he would write down immediately upon waking from this dream.

I stared out the window of my room at the city and its child-like populace, with its joyous blend of creation and wonder. A world erected by these people, I thought, would be a better one by far than the one Jehovah devised. But I knew that in such a world, I would find no place for myself, nor my peers, nor even Him, not when these free creatures embodied an immortality more vivid than ours could ever be.

Lucifer was at my side, wearing the body of a woman from the future, bedecked in celebrational regalia. "You're very brave, Gabriel," she said. "Doing what you know is right despite what you feel is right. Or are you doing what you feel is right despite what you know is right? Ah, to hell with it. Why must you be so unceasingly morose? Can't you see there's a party going on out there? Come on out. Live a little. I'll show you around."

" 'Tis indeed a beautiful city."

"Don't I know it. I am honestly amazed at this place. It's pretty nice during the day, of course, but at night this place opens up. I mean it really opens up. They take comers from all over time and space here. There's even a special embassy for dreamers. I can hardly believe what they've done with the second-rate world they've been given. You know how they do it? There's this guy that stood in the central square all day. Just stood there like a statue, not moving an inch, all day. So around dusk, a woman walks up, takes his place, and he starts living it up. I bought him a drink, asked him what he was doing all day. He said he was guiding the city's stream of consciousness. He said that bitterness, aggression, and malice were all just bits of an innocuous sludge that builds up over time, that they've got to be smoothed out after they happen or else they'll just sit there wherever the last user left them. I'm telling you, Gabriel, this town could inspire a Pharisee, or better yet, it could put a smile on Michael's face. How's the little guy doing, anyway?"

"As aflame for the duty that claims him here as I am reluctant."

"Oh, yeah, the Tower, I heard. When He puts another urban renewal project on the burner, word gets around. Must seem ridiculous to you, huh? Pointless. Sent all this way to ruin a perfectly happy way of life because of a building code. You find it a challenge to your faith, of course. Not in Him, but in yourself, am I right?"

"I have questioned the worth of my work since long before I arrived in this city. You know that better than any."

"Yeah, but you never stop, do you? That's why you're so gloomy all the time, my friend. Why not put it all aside for a moment? Yes, you have a duty, and there's no question that you will perform it to the letter, but where is the point in torturing yourself, Gabriel? You could learn a few things from the people here. They imagine differences here, but with the certainty that imagination is the only difference. And they realize that if you try to chop a block of wood across the grain, you'll only scar it."

"God's will shapes all things," Michael said, standing at the open doorway, his flaming sword half-drawn, his eyes smoking.

"Yes, Michael, but at what cost to the things themselves?" my friend asked somberly, never taking her gaze from the city outside the window.

"Ha, what do you know of cost, Fallen One, Pretender? When have you dealt with sacrifice? What have you relinquished, and for who? Only One knows the true price of all that is, and He weeps for it every day, every hour. But then what would you, a self-serving, indolent purveyor of falsehoods, care about the pain of others?"

Suddenly, Michael flew to the wall and remained flat against it, pinned by no hand, with a look of shock on his face. Lucifer, the light from her eyes now subdued, glided slowly towards my companion, her voice low and melodic, a melancholy tune, a dervish's death song. I looked on silently, unwilling to act in a scene I could not believe was unfolding. "Be glad, Michael, that my judgment is not as swift or irrevocable as His, or you would no longer have a tongue with which to make such pretty speeches. No one knows pain better than I. I am lord over all pain now, human and heavenly, and yes, even His. It is only my love for Him and His pain that drives me to act...at all." Michael and Lucifer were now inches apart, the impotent rage on my comrade's face absorbed slowly by the impassive and incalculable expression of Morningstar. "You have a job to do here, Michael. You must ensure this world's future. You also, friend Gabriel. Do your Lord's bidding." With a sudden breeze and a brief POP!, he was gone. Michael sank to the floor, then rose immediately to his feet, turning his flaming eyes on me. His hand moved to the hilt of his sword again. "You stood and did nothing," he said, the accusation plain.

I feigned nonchalance and turned my back to him. "He did not harm you, nor would he have for anything. 'Tis not his way." I closed my eyes, expecting the blow to come at any second.

"And how come you to be so familiar with his ways?" This time I heard the confusion. Lucifer's actions had left him bewildered and unsure, and like a spiteful child, his insinuation lacked conviction.

I gathered to myself the authority of time, layering the experience of eons through my voice, extra depth and breadth to my closest approximation of the Ultimate. "I know, youngling, because I fought beside him thousands of years before you were even an idea in the ether. I know because I have seen him many times threatened, browbeat, and set upon by impetuous children like yourself whom he could have crushed into dust effortlessly, yet not once has he been as ruthless as you. Leave, now. I wish to rest before we destroy this place."

He left without a word, still angry, but sufficiently cowed.

It was much later, after the Tower was gone and its people scattered and bewildered, relearning the ancient skills of fear and mistrust, that Michael and I ascended again.

The city of Heaven strikes the senses like light passing through a prism, its appearance dependent upon the shape and cleavage of the individual exposed. Lucifer had laughed good-naturedly at what he called Jehovah's ostentation, noting the golden gates rising beyond sight and the chambers and corridors, which extended forever in every direction. Michael would wander through these expanses like a child, his mouth agape in wonder. How could the same city, with the same sounds, strike me only as a place of fear? The gates, for instance, seem to loom over the applicant, reprimanding him with their purity, denying all justifications. No amount of begging or pleading or shouting or demanding budges them. Perhaps they open of their own inanimate wisdom, or maybe by a trick

of mechanical whim, but they are deaf and blind to reason. Once one makes it past the gates, Heaven continues to intimidate, as white light reflects and amplifies off every surface, obliterating every shadow and blinding the pilgrim's progress. Voices turned higher than a whisper bounce down the corridors, slip down side passages, and double back through improbable paths of chambers and hallways—gaining volume with every reverberation, but losing all nuance of tone—until, minutes later, the sound finally returns to the speaker in a painfully loud monotone, like the shouts of rocks. In Heaven, one looks down and speaks softly. Piety and humility meld with necessity.

As a rule, one did not meet Jehovah. He was a hermit in the reaches of infinity. He communicated directly only with a select few of His angels, who passed His commands down to lesser angels or made an appearance to humans. He had no friends, and Michael was His only protégé. This arrangement would have suited me had I not been one of those in His inner circle. I dreaded every meeting with Him. I feared His omniscience, the surety that He knew the confines of my heart thoroughly, that He saw my love was only terror redirected. I assumed every time I walked into His chamber would be the last; the judgment would come and I would be ripped asunder as some of the fallen ones had been. The summons after Babel was no exception.

I could not describe Him to you, for I have never seen His true face. Inside His chamber, Jehovah would appear as anything He wished, according to His own incomprehensible symbolism. When Michael and I entered after returning from the Tower, we found ourselves inside a vast and unlimited library, with rows upon rows of shelving disappearing into the distance, filled with millions of books yet to be written, all that could ever be known. I paused, unsure how to address Him in this form. Michael knew instinctually what was expected of him. He moved quickly to the nearest shelf and selected a book at random.

"My Father," he said, "we have returned, and the task You set before us is complete." He opened the book greedily, and a self-satisfied smile crept across his face.

I stepped to the aisle adjacent to his and pulled down a dusty red tome with no title printed. I opened to the first page, turned to the next, and flipped quickly through the rest of the book. I did the same with another volume from a higher shelf. "They are empty," I said, looking at Michael though not actually speaking to him. He simply smiled back. I looked again at the open book in my hand.

I AM HERE, read the bold type across the page which had been empty a moment before.

I held my expression still, engaging a reserve of quietude and a semblance of calm, a mask I used for my encounters with Him. "Have you looked upon our work which is Your work and seen it as good, My Lord?" I flipped to the next page.

IT IS GOOD, GABRIEL. WAST THOU UNSURE?

I paused, briefly, wording out my answer correctly in my mind despite the knowledge that He could observe this process as easily as if I were writing it down. "It is my place only to serve my Lord in His work, not to question it."

SO THOU WOULDST NEVER QUESTION ME, GABRIEL?

"I would not allow my questions to interfere with my service, my Lord." I winced. My answer had been immediate, without forethought, and it was the wrong one. As if to confirm this, the next page bore a condemnation.

ANOTHER WHO ONCE SERVED ME BELIEVED THAT. HE HAS SINCE FALLEN.

And then Michael spoke up, delivering the killing blow, "My Father, I no longer trust Gabriel. The night before the Tower fell, he consorted with the Adversary." No words appeared in my book, and I braced myself, waiting for the creative punishment He was sure to conjure to accompany my banishment from Heaven, sure that the axe was poised to fall, but Michael's agitation belied a response that I was not privy to.

"Then you must also know, My Father, of his inaction when the Fallen One attacked me," Michael argued. Still nothing appeared in my book. I was specifically not to know what Jehovah said to him, but whatever it was, Michael now took an air of solemn respect and said, "Yes, My Father. I await the opportunity to serve you further." He turned and left, ignoring me.

I waited silently in His chamber for many immeasurable lengths of time while my Lord brooded or mulled over or contemplated until I became certain he had forgotten my presence, but still I waited, unwilling to leave until my Lord dismissed me. Finally the strain of His presence threatened to dissipate me completely, and I asked timidly, "Is there anything further, my Lord?"

His voice resonated inside me immediately. WOULD YOU EVER HARM ME, GABRIEL, MY SERVANT?

"I do not believe I am able, my Lord." I needed no time to consider my words.

THEN YOU BELIEVE FALSELY, GABRIEL. WOULD YOU EVER HARM ME?

"Not if it were in my power to avoid doing so, my Lord."

IF I WERE TO PRESENT YOU WITH A TASK THAT WOULD CAUSE ME HARM, WHAT THEN?

I turned the question over in my mind, once, twice, examining it from every angle. It had to be a test, or simply a game. Perhaps it was a precursor to my punishment. No answer could be correct. Nothing assured my place or his appeasement. Giving in to fate, I decided on an answer as truthful as I knew.

"As I said, my Lord, my place is in service to You, and, though it remains untried, I am certain my powers do not extend to resistance of that duty. If my Lord wished for me to harm Him, I would have no choice but to do so, but not without misgivings." Once more I prepared myself for damnation, and once more He withheld it.

YOU WILL NEVER KNOW WHAT HARMS ME, GABRIEL, BUT NEVERTHELESS, YOU ARE SECOND ONLY TO ONE OF ALL OF MY SERVANTS.

I bowed nervously in thanks. "It is true, my Lord. None could exceed Michael in faith and devotion," I said, but the library had already disappeared, and His voice gave no reply.

I have seen history prove time and time again that, where a people has developed a wealth of any kind, be it material, cultural, or spiritual, there will come hordes of those who wish to wrest it from them. Practical men, upon hearing the true story of Babel, demand an explanation of how such a city could exist for so long without bringing down destruction from the aggressive nations surrounding it. They kept no army. They trained no soldiers. They sent no diplomats and abhorred the use of spies. Under threat of invasion, they made no preparations, changed nothing. They built no unwieldy fortifications. So how, it is asked, did they survive?

This is how.

When a hostile army appeared, bent on plunder and bloodshed, the entire populace—men, women, and children—all moved to the field outside the city and resumed what they had been doing inside, with one difference: they brought nothing with them. Blacksmiths continued pounding hot iron with hammers, except they had no iron and no hammer, only the movements of their well-toned chests and arms. Lovers engaged in a secret affair in a hidden garden would resume their consummations in the open. The back-and-forth exchanges of the marketplace went on as usual, only without the goods to trade hands. The entertainers performed without props; sword swallowers without their blades, the fire breathers spitting pure air, the musicians playing upon the instruments they had left behind, the dervishes whirling while the brightly colored scarves they would have twirled around themselves remained inside the city, folded neatly on the street. The children played their games without toys. The woman who wandered through the streets casting flowers continued tossing nothing into the field, and the love-struck young man devoted to her from afar followed inconspicuously behind her, gathering all those nothings into his arms.

With the context removed, the true meaning of their actions and lives became clear. The underlying rhythms and gracefully interwoven patterns of their movements became visible as the dance that they were.

The citizens of Babel feared no outside force because they believed so strongly in the complex beauty of their lives, and they knew that the day that they failed to reach *anyone* with their dance was the day the city would and should fall. They never failed.

Every invading force since the city's dawn had been moved to a standstill, shocked into reverie. Young warriors dropped their swords and laughed, suddenly aware of choices that had seemed impossible to them a moment before. Some veterans wept and fell upon their own weapons, unable to cope with all the time wasted killing and not living. Some ran to join the dance, the newest inhabitants of the city. Others simply turned and headed back towards their homelands, glad for their hands to be empty and clean of blood that day. Never was there any question of destroying such perfection.

And that is how, while civilizations floundered and crumbled and gave way to new cultures, while empires grew large and decayed, while cities and fields were razed again and again, Babel stood impervious and eternal, untouched by the violence of time. No one could see the true accomplishment of Babel and do it harm afterwards.

No one, that is, until Michael and I came.

We moved through the streets of Babel dressed as bandits, with the carriage of executioners. Faces and bodies hidden in the deep folds of our hooded robes, two drab gray figures, moving with the unmistakable bearing of the overtly righteous. Against our divinely bestowed presence, the city seemed out of place, like a tentative child unsure of whether or not it has committed some transgression.

It took a few seconds only for the inhabitants to notice us. As we drifted towards the Tower, I read the realization in their faces: all was not well in their house, catastrophe closed in, and the unthinkable was about to manufacture itself. They displayed fear, horror, bewilderment—and, in some, resignation to the end that comes to all things—but

one by one they fell in behind us, then two by two, then in the dozens and scores at once, some victims of our God-given grandeur, but most of them determined to prevent the atrocity we were bound to commit.

So began the final dream in the city of dreams. Two beings from parable led a procession of jugglers, troubadours, gardeners and carpenters, blacksmiths and contortionists, children with dirty feet, hard-eyed comedians brewing defiance, a proud old woman poised for battle, a subtly terrified young stable hand, the troll from the caravan, a shepherd projecting a peaceful confidence. A stone-faced procession filtered out from the doorways and side streets and climbed down from the balconies and the trees, aware that their celebration of life was coming to an end. A crowd with suicidal intentions and straightforward courage.

We arrived in the square before the Tower, moved to a position in the center, and waited for the crowd to gather around us. When they encircled us completely, a mass of melancholy expectation, Michael acted. His robe began to smolder along his shoulder blades. Two slow tendrils of smoke rose, and suddenly his entire robe fell to pieces, engulfed in flames. The crowd made no reaction to his display, staring as the vaguely humanoid conflagration sprouted wings of fire, which flapped quickly once, twice, and propelled him into the air. Thirty feet in the air he hovered, looking down at the Babelites looking back at him, still silenced in their dread. Then he spoke:

"Citizens of the city of Babel. We are arrived to redress a great sin. A sin committed by every man, woman, and child of this city. You have thought your city the most beautiful in all of existence. And you have, in your pride, erected a passage into the heavens, which any may travel regardless of

God's wishes. You have rejected Him and His words in favor of your own. You have forgotten to whom all is indebted. You have angered your Lord with your shortsighted arrogance and your irreverent vanity. We are God's wrath made flesh. We are God's judgment brought down from Heaven. Behold, as the works of your sins are laid low, one by one, by the hand of your Lord."

I despised his theatrics and I despised him for his self-importance. I was revolted to be a part of it, but I remained unshaken in my resolve. As the city did indeed look on, Michael, with the smallest movement of his hand, ripped the Tower up from its foundations. No rumbling, no quaking, just the brief sound of rocks crashing, and then it floated in the air thirty feet above where it had stood. The people were still, the machines were silent, and all the animals in the city had already left. Michael crackled lightly like burning wood above us all, and I prepared for my part.

With a flamboyant gesture, Michael started the Tower spinning in the air like a work wheel, slowly at first, then, under his manipulation, it picked up speed, rotating faster and faster, until the features of the carvings blurred beyond distinction. Michael shouted, and a stream of fire sprang from his wing to the Tower, which it began to climb and circle like ivy. It branched out once, then the separate branches split and split again from those shoots. Each strand crossed another, and the web eventually reached the top and doubled back down until, finally, a white-hot and blinding net of fire enfolded the Tower completely, masking it from view. With a final nudge, Michael sent the Tower into a cycle of infinite momentum, spinning it until its pieces broke off from the centrifugal force. As they were cast, they flew through the net of fire and ignited, sent away past the horizon, speck after flaming speck disappearing out of sight.

At the same time that Michael first sent the Tower spinning, the citizens began the dance, simultaneously springing into the steps of their lives. Inspired now by their loss, they transformed the ritual from an expression of celebration to a conduit of tragedy. They performed the eulogy for their home. And as they did, I stepped into their midst, physically and mentally, infusing myself with their group consciousness, becoming, in effect, one of them, another line in their pattern. As I moved among them, I wiped from their minds, one by one, the knowledge and memories of that language that was never spoken or heard, only shown and seen. Some had spent their entire lives with that perfect understanding, and I obliterated it in a few seconds. I did not hesitate, nor did I falter at their reactions. The language was an object, a sickness to be eliminated by the swift, surgical thrusts of my mind into theirs. In my wake, I left a trail of fear and bewilderment. Strange, wide-eyed creatures of terror and territory, suffering and retribution—frantically suspicious, they searched each other for the recognition which they would not find. They froze like rabbits, cut off from the dance that grew smaller with every human I touched. Like insects throwing themselves against glass, their thoughts battered against the walls of my mind, never penetrating, but leaving their stains. "How could I trust him?" "Where did they go?" "If you don't stop that, so help me, I'll…." "Please don't leave me alone." "I want to die." Separated from each other by all the differences they could imagine.

All told, the destruction of the Tower and the demoralization of its people took no more than half of an hour, though it seemed less. There is no need to recount the razing of the city or the scattering of its inhabitants, although, rest assured, it was completed just as efficiently.

It was the same with hundreds of other places more or less deserving. None ever really had a chance. Fire poured down, earthquakes rattled their fear-stained seconds, the bright white lightning of His "perfect love" charred landscapes exotic and irretrievable, and no one could offer resistance. Always, I watched, with my power and my impotence. I stood by and viewed myself make it all happen. Now that it's over, now that they're, ev'ry one, gone, Jehovah, Michael, even Lucifer, forgotten or dispatched, I can tell these stories and finish sealing myself in this past. Long past now, covered in shadow is my era. I am the translucent remnant.

Dedicated to Matt, for constantly reminding me that I am just another monkey, and to Push, for constantly demonstrating to me what monkeys are capable of.

SLEEPING GHOSTS

Cut the darkness
  with a flashlight's
    straight
    and narrow beam.
  Dust in the attic
    where once trunks
      stored the trinkets
        which trigger memories
      instead of footsteps,
      instead of faces.
The attic ghosts
  have faded,
    barely echoes
    of an unknown past.
Not every memory
  is pleasant,
  not every ghost
    kind.
Dream of me
  in the darkness
    in the attic
    leaving footsteps
      in the dust.
      Hear me whisper,
        feel my tears
        roll fresh
          under your eyes.
The attic ghosts
  have faded,
  let us lie.

—John Urbancik

AN INTERVIEW WITH DOUGLAS CLEGG

By Michael McCarty

Born in Alexandria, Virginia, but having shared space in Hawaii, Connecticut, Washington DC, California, and other places that he has already forgotten, Douglas Clegg is getting around.

He began writing in his late twenties and already has nine published novels, including Goat Dance, The Children's Hour, *and* The Halloween Man, *as well as thirty-five short stories. His latest is* The Nightmare Chronicles, *published by Leisure Books.*

Clegg has worked as a teacher, editor, journalist, and bum. He is a graduate of Washington & Lee University with a B.A. in English Literature, a survivor of the Los Angeles riots, has lived through one mother of an earthquake, and has survived a near-crash in a jet. He is married and lives where no stalker can find him. He has a border collie mutt named Randy and a tailless black cat named Sophie.

DP: Why do you write horror?

DC: I write horror because it seems to be my perspective, at least fictionally. Writing novels is really what I do—and some novels of mine may not be called horror, some will. I just write what I write, and I don't really think about genre, nor do I sit down to write a horror novel. I just sit down to tell a story, and the stories thus far have come from a horror perspective.

DP: Did you always want to write, or was it something you sort of fell into and liked?

DC: I knew I would write fiction for a living since I was about nine years old, when I began typing out stories. Most of them I kept hidden because I knew they weren't right. I began writing nonfiction and editing for a living in my early twenties, and I didn't finish a novel until I was about twenty-eight, and this novel was *Goat Dance*, which came out in 1989. I still edit and write nonfiction, too—these are the things I

enjoy doing, so I just go with it.

DP: What is the hardest part of being a professional novelist?

DC: The hardest part is the galleys—I hate this stage in writing when I see all the flaws in a book and must figure out how to love a book again after I've spent years writing or thinking about it. Frankly, I don't think there's a hard part to being a professional novelist; the hard stuff for me would be wondering what people do who don't write. Life would seem empty to me without it, it would be like life without music.

DP: Can you give us a sneak-peek at your upcoming novel, *You Come When I Call You*?

DC: Sure. It's a big, sprawling novel of four teenagers growing up in 1980 on the high desert of California, and the demon that ends up possessing them. The story follows them for twenty years as the horror within them continues in one way or another. It's also a bit of a tenement cathedral of a novel—an unsound structure, full of secret chambers and corridors that lead to precipices. As with *The Halloween Man*, rather than go with linear and chronological reality, I followed the psychological reality of the four main characters. I have been writing and revising (and cutting) this novel for over a decade, which means I have no perspective on it. It might suck; it might be good. But I do think that it's a kind of horror novel that no one is writing at the moment, and I hope readers enjoy the experience.

DP: On the same line, that book took you ten years to write. Why?

DC: Well, mainly because I really didn't want to publish it. It feels like the novel of my life, yet it doesn't resemble my life much. I wanted to create—don't laugh—a cathedral of a novel, a cubist novel, a story that could be moved forward or back through and still all the elements could be picked up. I actually believe you could read this novel backwards and still maintain suspense and momentum. Perhaps I'm insane. Originally, *You Come When I Call You* reached a maximum of two thousand pages, but this was because I was living in the book. I destroyed relationships around it; then I grasped what was more central to the story, and I brought it down into readability. Plus, I was writing other novels, too, so I'd set the book aside for six months at a time. And I think I needed to mature before I could see the story clearly. The ten years helped. Writing other fiction helped. I wasn't ready to serve the vision I had of this story when I was twenty-eight and began writing it. I never thought a novel would take so much of my life; it almost hurts to let it go.

DP: Do you think you'll ever venture into another genre?

DC: Maybe; I really can't predict this. I go where the story takes me, and if one day I come up with a romance or a science fiction tale, then I'll follow where the story leads. The only label I want is "storyteller." The story is the most important thing; someday I'll be dead, and the story will still either exist or not, without my being there. I'm just a servant (and not a humble one—I love being able to tell tales.)

DP: Do you have any other novels in the works now?

DC: Always. I'm working on *Mischief*, a novel which comes out in the fall of 2000, as well as doing research on hauntings for its prequel, an e-mail novel I'm sending out (as I did *Naomi* in the summer of 1999) during the summer and early fall of 2000. The prequel is called "Nightmare House," and is about a haunting on a grand scale. People can sign up by going to my web page at www.douglasclegg.com and adding themselves to the "list," or by just e-mailing me with a note to subscribe to the Douglas Clegg list at DClegg@douglasclegg.com. And it's free—a free horror novel via e-mail. A bargain!

DP: What was the inspiration for *Neverland*?

DC: When I was a bit younger, I went with a friend and his family to their summer place on Sea Island, Georgia. The place—desolate but beautiful at the time—had a profound effect on me. But my main inspiration was that I wanted to detail how I felt about childhood's perspective, and then the horror just came through. There is a bit of a homage to "Sredni Vashtar" if you look for it in that novel—the story by Saki, one of my favorite writers.

DP: In *The Nightmare Chronicles*, you said in the dedication that writing is like being held hostage. What does that mean?

DC: Storytelling is a form of kidnapping. I really believe that if the story is right, then the reader is captive. It's a way of drawing attention into another world—kidnapping the reader into another realm of experience. I like that about stories.

DP: What sort of reactions do you get from people when you tell them what you do for a living?

DC: I don't tell too many people. Generally, when people find out, I don't get any interesting reactions—I wish I had a better answer, but it's the truth. Americans generally don't care about writers

unless the writer just signed a $100 million deal, then suddenly Tom Clancy becomes a fascinating person. Luckily, we all care about stories. Stories feed us. So I'll let Clancy have the interest at cocktail parties, and I'll just keep writing stories, which are always more important than writers, anyway.

DP: You published *Bad Karma* under a pseudonym. Why? And was it hard to take—being a best-seller when the book is not in your own name (á la Dean Koontz syndrome)?

DC: I wrote *Bad Karma* under a pseudonym mostly for the fun of it. I wanted to try a different kind of novel, a mainstream thriller, brutal though it was. I wanted to indicate to readers of my supernatural horror novels that this was a bit different. I believe that *Bad Karma* will be re-released under my own name at some point. It really was a lark, but for some reason, everyone wanted to know if I was hiding or if I was changing direction permanently. Neither of the two. I just wanted to try a different name.

DP: What was the first horror and science fiction story you remember reading as a child that had an impact on you?

DC: Well, the first horror story was no doubt either "Daniel and the Lion's Den" or that one about the men walking through the furnace in the Bible. Maybe the plagues of Egypt. The Bible has some great horror in it. Then, probably my mom reading Poe to me as a little kid didn't hurt. The first science fiction novel I ever read was by Dean Koontz. I had no idea who wrote it at the time, but, years later, when I read the biography of Dean by Katherine Ramsland, there was the title (*The Fall of the Ream Machine*, I believe was the name.) So Dean, who has been a mentor and an extremely generous individual to me and other novelists, also happens to have been one of the first popular novelists I ever read. I was probably eleven or twelve when I read the book. I remember it to this day, having never seen it again.

DP: *The Nightmare Chronicles* features thirteen of your stories (about half of those you have published.) Do you think there will be another collection in the future?

DC: I want another collection, but the problem with getting collections out in mass market is that publishers tend to be leery. Novels sell better, and a publisher's business is to sell books. But I do have one ready to go, called "The Machinery of Night." Perhaps, if I'm lucky, a small press publisher will pick it up. Who knows? I tend not to market myself all that much (despite appearances, I don't have an agent), so I pretty much wait until some editor contacts me and then I just say, "Yep, I got something for ya." This is not the smartest way to run a career—so for aspiring writ-

Frankly, I don't think there's a hard part to being a professional novelist. The hard stuff for me would be wondering what people do who don't write.

ers out there, ignore this method. It just works for me. I'm sure Tom Clancy doesn't do this. I doubt that Michael Crichton does either.

DP: Who are some of your favorite horror and science fiction writers?

DC: Ah, if I tell, I'll leave someone off. Let me just say what I've recently been reading: I enjoy Bentley Little's novels a great deal, and beyond the megasellers, most of whom I love, I like Christopher Golden's stuff, a writer named Boston Teran's novel *God is a Bullet*, Elizabeth Engstrom's dark fiction, pretty much anything by Elizabeth Hand…a recent novel called *Something Dangerous* by a newer writer from England, Patrick Redmond, caught my attention because it is set in a boy's school, as is my upcoming novel, *Mischief*—happily,

Something Dangerous is a very different kind of novel, and quite brilliant.

DP: Was *The Breeder* turned into a movie?

DC: Nope, no movies thus far, although *The Children's Hour* now has a screenplay from the director of *Hellraiser II* and *III* and may be in production shortly. *Bad Karma* was optioned, as was my short story, "The Mysteries of Paris." I think there were several cheesy horror movies called *The Breeder* or *Breeders*. It's a popular title, I guess. I'm pretty sure my book came first (in 1990, although it was written and in to my publisher in 1988.)

DP: Any last words?

DC: Just wanted to thank readers for sticking with me for *The Halloween Man*, *The Nightmare Chronicles*, *Naomi*, and I hope, *You Come When I Call You*. I would like to add that the editor's role in all this is rarely mentioned, so I have to mention the people who have taught me much about writing and stories: Linda Marrow, my editor at Pocket; Jacob Hoye, my editor at Dell; Don D'Auria, my editor at Leisure; Sky Nonhoff, my editor in Germany; Rich Chizmar, my editor at CD Publications; Ellen Datlow, one of the best editors for horror and science fiction and fantasy in this country. I wish she were at a major publishing house. She would really bring in the books! These are only the editors I've worked with; there certainly are other wonderful ones out there. I wanted to shine a little light on them, since I could not do what I do without them.

-dp-

CONTRIBUTORS

Between them, **John Benson** and **Tina Riegel** have had more than eighty poems accepted for publication in such magazines as *The Urbanite, Palace Corbie, The Third Alternative, Grue, Tales of the Unanticipated,* and *Contortions.* John does survey research in Boston, and Tina works for a pharmaceutical company in North Carolina. They collaborate on their poetry by e-mail and phone.

Bruce Boston is the author of twenty five books and chapbooks, including the novel Stained Glass Rain. His stories and poems have appeared in hundreds of publications, including *Asimov's, Amazing Stories, Realms of Fantasy, Weird Tales, Year's Best Fantasy and Horror,* the *Pushcart Prize Anthology,* and five *Nebula Awards* anthologies. His fiction and poetry collection, *The Complete Accursed Wives,* is forthcoming Dark Regions. In 1999, the Science Fiction Poetry Association honored him with the only Grand Master Award presented in its twenty-two year history.

M.L.Ching has lived for twenty-one years. He tentatively plans to continue doing so for a few more. He is mostly water, but he tries not to neglect the 9% of himself that is carbon.

G. O. Clark lives/works in Davis CA with a teen son and a cat. His poems have appeared in *Asimov's, Talebones, Star*Line, PirateWritings, Manhattan Poetry Review, California Quarterly,* and

many other magazines over the last 20 years. He's been nominated for the Rhysling Award a couple of times, and regularly reviews books and magazines for *Star*Line.* He has two out of print chapbooks under collar, *Letting The Eye To Wonder & Seven Degrees of Something.*

David M. Cox is a sometime writer and erstwhile editor living Southern California. He has worked at jobs that vary from slinging videos to legwork at a private investigations firm. His own fiction has appeared in *After Hours* and in *Tales of the Unanticipated,* for whom he was an associate editor from 1996 to 1998. He now handles new business for a large insurance company. In his spare time and long into the night, he edits and publishes that unparalleled publication you're reading right now, *Darkling Plain Speculative Fiction.* Thanks for reading.

Denise Dumars has published three collections of poetry and one of fiction. She currently covers horror and science fiction novels, television, and movies for Fandom.Com, *Cinefantastique* and *Femme Fatales,* in addition to writing articles on Wicca and related subjects for Llewellyn Publications and assorted New Age magazines. Her short stories are appearing in *The Edge: Tales of Suspense* and in the *BBR Anthology.* Her poetry is currently published in *Edgar: Digested Verse* and *Dreams of Decadence.* She is editing the poetry anthology *Isis Rising: The Goddess in the New Aeon* for the Temple of Isis Los Angeles.

Rhonda Eikamp writes, "I'm originally from Garland, Texas, and live with my husband and daughter in Germany where I work as a translator. Stories of mine have appeared in *The Urbanite, Talebones, The Silver Web* and, most recently, *Indigenous Fiction.* As to "That Moves My Bones," I really did write the story before *Shakespeare In Love.*

Eric M. Heideman is a Minneapolis children's librarian. He has published fiction in *Writers of the Future, Volume III; Alfred Hitchcock's Mystery Magazine;* and *Best Mystery and Suspense Stories, 1988* (Walker), and over 125 reviews and features (mostly SF-related) in the Minneapolis Star Tribune and other periodicals. In his spare time, he has edited the Minnesota Science Fiction Society's semiprozine, *Tales of the Unanticipated* (TOTU) since 1986, and since 1982 has done lots of committee work for Twin Cities-area SF conventions, including Diversicon and Arcana. He also moderates a SF book-discussion group, Second Foundation, hosts SF Minnesota's monthly Speculations Readings Series at DreamHaven Books, and coordinates an annual fall video party surveying the history of the classic horror film. This spring sees the publication of TOTU #21, as well as his first book, *Somehow it Fits: The Tales of the Unanticipated Interviews* (Stone Dragon Press). He lives in a co-op apartment building overlooking a park with a lake, in company with his faithful phone-answering cats,

Benjamin Disraeli II and Sarah Jane Smith.

Of his artwork, cover artist **Phil Hoffman** writes, "the shapes in these works evoke forms and objects found in the real world. The artist maintains that each person will have their own set of interpretations drawn from their own experiences upon viewing them. This invokes an active creative association between the viewer and the paintings. The titles are a starting point for the process as the images are engaged in the mind of the viewer, involving a personal associative/creative response. It is the essential intent of the artist to provoke the viewer into a creative state of mind."

Bruce Horton is a professional illustrator who specializes in fantasy and science fiction art. His work has been published in newspaper editorials and software company advertising materials. Bruce's work is quite diversified and covers a wide area of the illustrative field. In addition to fantasy and science fiction art, Bruce also creates original cartoons, historical and military illustration, as well as wildlife art.

Pam Keesey has edited three collections of short stories, *Daughters of Darkness*, *Dark Angels*, and *Women Who Run with the Werewolves*. She is also the author of *Vamps: An Illustrated History of the Femme Fatale*. Her essay, "*The Haunting* and the Power of Suggestion" will be appearing in the *Horror Film Reader*, edited by James Ursini

and Alain Silver in the Spring of 2000.

H. Courreges LeBlanc doesn't recall being born in New Orleans—he was very young at the time. But it must have been traumatic, since afterwards he didn't speak for a year. He's been writing for as long as he can remember, but the trouble really started when he went to Clarion in 1996. Since then, he's sold four short stories and written a novel called "The Tainted Cotillion," full of talking rats, zombie Confederates, nymphomaniac debutantes, and detachable penises. The novel is in the hands of a Tor editor and an otherwise reputable agent, who are taking more than the usual precautions. In addition to his literary crimes, there are also certain (so-called) musical offenses for which he must eventually answer. However, despite numerous live appearances and recordings showing up on film, television, and radio, LeBlanc has evaded apprehension. Perhaps it's going too far to say that he's made fools of the proper authorities, but they certainly look forward to his arrest and conviction. Even his name is deviant-"H. Courreges LeBlanc." What kind of name is "Courreges?" No one has the faintest notion how to pronounce it. It's far too ethnic, and even vaguely dirty. And what lurks beneath that cryptic "H?" This man is a menace, and he must be stopped at all costs.

Cindy Rako is a resident of Minnesota who enjoys doing illustrations for horror and dark

fantasy stories as a break from the real-life horror stories she deals with in her job with the City Prosecutor's Office.

Jo-Ann Lamon Reccoppa works as a correspondent for Greater Media Newspapers. Her first love is dark fiction, however, and her short stories have appeared in publications such as *Aberrations* and *Shadowdance*. She both a past treasurer and a member in good standing of the Garden State Horror Writers in New Jersey.

Patricia Russo does a plethora of odd jobs, none of which she dares put on her resume. Currently scribing, learning ASL, and writing in snatched moments.

Ann K. Schwader's poetry has appeared in *Time Frames* (Rune Press,) *The Nyarlathotep Cycle*, *The Innsmouth Cycle* (both Chaosium Press,) *Weird Tales*, *Space & Time*, and elsewhere in the small and pro press. She is an active member of both SFWA and HWA.

Given **Robert Subiaga, Jr.**'s undergraduate education in neurophysiology, his graduate education in philosophy, his endless obsession with the mind-body problem, and his seven-year stint doing neurological research, you might be tempted to believe parts of the short story published in this issue are based on real events. Nothing could be further from the truth. Subiaga, for example, never has had sex with any real corpses. Only Lutherans.

Billy Tackett is a self-taught, freelance artist/illustrator born and raised in northeastern and now living in the Cincinnati, Ohio area. He specializes in fantasy and horror but also does commissioned portraits and classic car "portraits." He has done several book covers, magazine illustrations and CD covers.

Marcie Lynn Tentchoff lives in the small town of Gibsons, BC, Canada, with various animals and the rest of her rather odd family. Her fiction and poetry have sold to various magazines and anthologies including *On Spec, Dreams of Decadence, Weird Tales,* and *Altair.* Marcie is poetry editor for *Spellbound,* the new fantasy magazine for young and preteens. She loves feedback and can be reached at marcie_tentchoff @sunshine.net.

John Urbancik lives in the shadow of The Mouse in Orlando, Florida, where the sun broils his flesh and the moon chills his mind. He writes fantasy (dark and light,) children's stories, and not-for-children stories. His stories and poetry have appeared in a list of places, including *Cemetery Sonata, Flesh & Blood,* and *Dreams of Decadence.* In his spare time, he rearranges Magnetic Poetry and collects colors.

Augie Wiedemann began illustrating for magazines in the early '80s. His horror fantasies have appeared in numerous magazines including *Deathrealm, Bizarre Bazaar, Thin Ice, Grue, Not One Of Us, Space & Time,* and *Tales Of The Unanticipated,* plus a small number of books such as *Quick Chills II.*

Chris Whitlow is a self taught artist who grew up on the gulf coast with a love for science fiction, fantasy and horror. After many years of travel throughout the world, he now lives in Florida with his wife, daughter, and a cat named Gravity. His first awards were for safety posters for the Navy, and he has gone on to win recognition in juried shows throughout the U.S. He has done commercial work and fine art, which has been mostly portraiture. He has published work throughout the small presses in *Odyssey, Talebones, Pulp Eternity, Challenging Destiny, Space and Time,* and others. His award-wining work hangs in professional buildings and private collections around the world. He has worked in all mediums, but his favorite mediums are still pencil and watercolor.

Connie Wilkins lives in the 5-college area of western Massachusetts, where she co-owns two stores supplying the non-essential necessities of student life. In the past few years she's had stories in publications ranging from *Marion Zimmer Bradley's Fantasy Magazine* through two of Bruce Coville's children's anthologies to Daw Books' *Prom Night,* along with some online and small press appearances and a few forays into other genres, in some cases pseudonymously. Stories will be coming soon in *Such a Pretty Face: Tales of Power and Abundance from Meisha* Merlin Press, and *100 Crafty Little Cat Tales* from Barnes & Noble.

Frank Wu is a science fiction illustrator, amateur paleontologist, kitsch-meister and patent agent living in Mountain View, California. His artwork has previously appeared in various publications including the Australian print science-fiction magazine *Altair* and in the e-zine *E-scape.* He recently won the L. Ron Hubbard Illustrators of the Future contest. His website is at www.frankwu.com. Email him at fwu@frankwu.com and ask him about his favorite nudibranchs.

-dp-

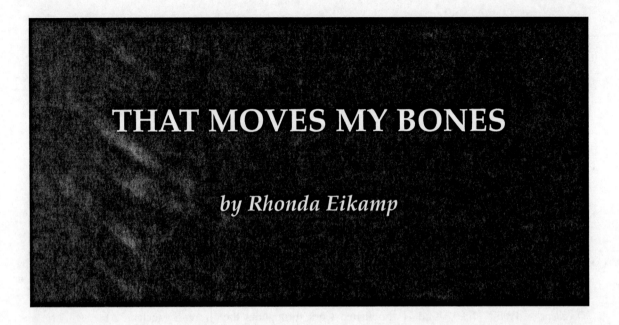

THAT MOVES MY BONES

by Rhonda Eikamp

My partner got that look on his face that meant the call was important. The read-out on my screen said it was being piped through the Well—a Jumper, maybe with information. I leaned across the desk, and Clyde tongued out of the transmission long enough to whisper, "It's the woman who stole Shakespeare."

When opportunity calls, you Jump. I was filling out the Jump request before Clyde could finish nodding and uh-huhing. While he talked, he keyed a message to my screen: she's saying he didn't make any difference she wants to give him back.

Others had stopped work—the click of keyboards and murmurs fading—to watch us. Todd Gordon smirked. "Big case?" His desk was next to mine, and the smell of hate rose off him. Because of our backgrounds, Clyde and I were scum, something less than human. Like vultures, they were waiting for us to screw up a case.

"Don't get your boxers in a wad," I told him, slotted the Jump request, and tongued into Sanchez's virtual office.

Lieutenant Sanchez had rigged his program to blot out his face. It was an intimidation tactic that worked on rookies. I watched the ball of fog on his shoulders study my Jump request.

"Who is Shakespeare again?" he said.

"You got the file."

"I don't need a file. I need to know is he important." I cursed the program that prevented me from seeing his eyes. I like to look a man in the eyes. Especially when he's about to shoot me down.

"You two Jump a lot, don't you? What was it, three times last month? You think it's the wild west out there. You, especially."

The panorama window behind Sanchez showed a real-time view of L.A. I saw the light of the noon sky flicker off and on, a power brown-out in the Cube that covered the city and kept Chinese Europe from

attacking us. The Cube hadn't been there before Shakespeare was stolen from our past. That's what our Well informants said, and I believed them. As soon as the writings—and the memory—of the man left us, the feeble chain of cause and effect broke and formed new links, and the end of that new chain was a war we wouldn't have to endure if we could only get him back.

Sanchez's problem was that he didn't have any imagination. Those who Jumped and returned saw the world change. They alone remembered what had been. That scared people like Sanchez. During a Jump two years ago, I shot and killed a man about to cut my head off with a laser, and Sanchez used the incident to brand me as trigger-happy. His report concluded that Clyde and I shouldn't be allowed to Jump as often. It was his way of hog-tying us.

"I like to Jump," I said. His hands shuffled the Shakespeare file nervously. "So does my partner. Does that bother you? We get the job done."

"One shot fired and you never Jump again. You got that?" I nodded. "Now get out."

I tongued out and was once again sitting across from Clyde. Clyde's eyes sparkled. He was like a kid sometimes. I decided not to tell him about the no-shot rule.

"The perp's name is Mercy," he told me. "She fed me the Well coordinates where she wants us to meet her. She has Billy Boy in her own world's past, London, 1592. She's bent on giving him back, John, but there's a problem." Clyde leaned forward. The sparkle in his eyes threatened to explode. "A third world's dropped in."

"What?"

"They want Billy for themselves. They've apparently sent a whole troop of Jumpers to Mercy's world to take him before she can give him back to us."

"Thieves stealing from the thief."

"She's holed up at the coords with him. They're surrounded. We'll have to bust them out."

Fighting over Shakespeare. I knew the Bard was a one-off phenomenon. None of the other worlds we had visited had one. Still, it seemed they were going to a lot of trouble for one little guy in stockings.

"They must all think he's really something," I muttered. Clyde shrugged.

An incoming message scrolled across my retinals. It was the Jump approval with Sanchez's signature. The man had come through. I felt the pervasive quiet that webbed the workroom, the eyes not watching us. "Got your gun, pardner?" Clyde nodded. "Let's move 'em out."

Down we went into the heart of Chronocriminology, past dimly lit basement rooms crammed with moldering police paraphernalia from another century. The Well room lay hidden behind a blank door that looked like a broom closet and swung onto a softly lit chamber. Technicians studied centerfolds over the controls or drank ersatz coffee. Laid back, they called it. Asleep at the ninth wonder of the world. The one that I handed our approval shrugged, then motioned us toward the center.

With all those newts' tongues and cauldrons boiling, Shakespeare could have written about the Well. The pool of fog where the floor ended—ended as in ceased to exist—writhed under amber light, punctuated by minute lightning bolts like the filigree of an inked fingerprint. Bubbles as black as bruises broke from the surface. The stench of ozone burned my nostrils. A constant roar rose from the Well, a heaving orchestra of the worlds that lay within: storms, shouts, cannons, jets, infants, earthquakes, lovers—every sound history uses to lasso itself into place. Don't think it wasn't scary. Looking down into the pool, I could understand why the regular cops hated Clyde and me. Either we had a courage they lacked, or something was missing from us, the sense of solidity that bound non-Jumpers to this world and wouldn't let them leave it.

Clyde gave the coordinates to the technician and stood beside me at the edge of the abyss. He was grinning like a puppy. The technician gave us the thumbs-up, and we Jumped.

Claws gouged my mind. It was like fighting an eagle, the feathery beat against my shirt, the caress of a wild animal, and lancing through it all—pain and terror. I felt the interstices where no world grew, where there was no human thought to cling to…then ground rose to slap me, cold dewed grass. I rolled, spat out dirt and stood.

Wherever I land in the past, the air always takes my breath away. Unnoticeable, the way it's meant to be. A sweet nothing. I stood on a hill in a sullen dawn, spring or fall, looking down across Renaissance London, or what passed for it in this world. From a thousand chimneys rose meager coal smoke. Shadows of early risers crept through the streets. My breath steamed. I turned at a gurgling sound beside me and saw Clyde eject. The Well manifested in the receiving world as a glittering, cone-shaped distortion that only stayed stable long enough to spit us out. The point of the cone wavered as the technicians made adjustments, and then it blinked out. It wouldn't open again until we signaled them. We were on our own. Clyde stood and checked the relays on his belt. "In there."

For the first time, I noticed the structure behind us, a three-tiered, roofless stadium of weatherbeaten wood, with a barn-door entrance and slits for windows. It looked exactly like a huge, lidless bowl dropped on the grass. In our world it would have been the Swan or the Globe. The perp had stolen Shakespeare from us just before he began to write his most famous works in London. It made sense that she would bring him to a similar theater here in her own past, to encourage him to write the works for her world that he would have written for ours. The theater stood deserted in the early hours.

"Let's do it," I said. We started toward it.

A low earth wall, overgrown with blue columbine, ran around the theater, the remnant of an older ring theater on the same site. As we topped the ridge and started for the entrance, exposed to the scores of high viewing slits that made the theater as ominous as a fortress, I realized my mistake. A flash burst from one of the slits. Not laser, I had time to think. The pain hit my shoulder and spun me around, tightened steel bands on my throat. Something was wrong with my head. I could hear Clyde shouting as he dragged me back behind the earthworks, my face in columbine, and I was falling….

Bright Iowa corn. I lay in corn, staring up at a sky so blue my eyes hurt. The shock of it galvanized me. I was home. True home, as though all the Jumps I had ever made had rewound back down to this point. And abruptly the shock turned to calm. So what if I was? Clyde, all of it, gone. Hadn't it all been like a bad dream? Leaving Iowa for L.A. so long ago, years looking for fame Hollywood-style, until the man—my recruiter—showed up one day in my shabby apartment. Instead of fame, I'd found a chronocop job, and what was that? Shards of worlds, no world my own. Somewhere far away, my shoulder ached. I had a job to do. None of it mattered. In a moment Pa would come and tell me to get my lazy self up. Wind shook the corn.

"John." Clyde knelt beside me, staring down. The sky was too clear, even for Iowa. The pain in my shoulder had vanished. I felt vague, not all there. "It's the third party complicating the handover," Clyde said. "They have the entire theater. I don't know what they're shooting with. Some beam. It only strafed you for a second, but you…faded. I could see through you."

The vision of the farm still caught at my blind spot, green….I sat up and swallowed the dizziness. "Whatever they're shooting sets up some field that neutralizes Jumps. Best I can figure. It sent me back. I imagine a longer shot would have made it permanent." He was nodding. He hadn't understood. "All the way back, Clyde. I was in my original timeline."

"The original?" He sat back, stunned. I knew what he was thinking. "God, John, I can't go back there! I just can't."

"Then don't get shot."

Thunder rumbled over the theater. We turned to look. A cone of glistening lights—the largest Well end node I had ever seen—appeared in the sky long enough to spew uniformed figures through the roofless lid of the building. Moments later, the soldiers appeared at ground level, guarding the doorway. In the half light, their skin looked green. We ducked behind the embankment.

"Reinforcements," Clyde said. "They must want him bad."

I turned and studied the bottom of the hill where London began: weed-etched lanes, scattered cottages, an inn. In front of the inn stood a brewer's wagon, the dray horses chomping grass while their master tended to business inside.

"She said she'd hole up with Shakespeare in the alcove behind the stage," Clyde murmured. "They aren't attacking because they're afraid of hurting him. We could go in shooting and not stop till we have him."

That was Clyde's standard solution. I thought of Sanchez's hands clenching the file. He had meant what he said. "I have a better idea." I said, and pointed to the inn. It took Clyde a moment to realize what I meant.

He moaned. "Not again. What is it with you and horses?"

I spoke quietly as we unharnessed the drays.

"The embankment'll hide our approach. Elizabethan theaters were arenas with dirt floors where the poor stood. We can ride in the door and straight up to the stage."

"They'll shoot the horses out from under us."

From the lane beyond the inn came a coughing, sputtering sound. Oddly familiar, yet I couldn't place it. We had no time to think about it. Faces had appeared at the inn's upper windows. "No one shoots horses," I told him. I swung up. "At least they don't in the movies."

"These guys are genetically altered, John. You saw them. They're lizards. Hell knows what their branch of the future looks like. They probably don't know what horses are."

"Too late." The brewer had appeared at the door. He shouted and started toward us. "Move 'em out, pardner!"

The horses were like locomotives. Slow to start, but once their piston legs were pumping, brick walls wouldn't have stopped them. The lizard men weren't brick walls. They howled as we crested the ridge—not quite human howls—and scattered back into the theater. Some turned to shoot, aiming low. So much for not shooting horses. Clyde's mount swerved and screamed as a rosebud of bundled light exploded against its right foreleg. Whatever effect the shots had on creatures in their own timeline, it hurt.

Then I was through the barn-door entrance and galloping toward the stage that projected into the arena. A marquee above the stage welcomed me to the Alchimical Carriage Theatre. Along the inner walls hung tiers of boxed seats intended for the rich. More shots flashed from the boxes as the lizard men climbed to vantage points. I heard another scream, not a horse this time. I reached the stage, vaulted from my horse, and came up running. The stage was open, no curtains in Elizabeth's day, only a door leading to backstage. I turned in time to see Clyde leap from his injured horse just before it tripped and rolled. He landed on the stage. Something in his movements was wrong.

"Go on," he yelled. I threw open the backstage door.

Somehow I hadn't expected young. The perp named Mercy huddled against the back wall of an alcove filled with stage props, lit by a single slit window at the back. She pointed a gun at the entrance. I hadn't expected beautiful. Silver hair, like clouds glimpsed at twilight. Desert-golden eyes, wide with fright. A dead lizard lay in front of her.

"You called—" I started to say, when Clyde rammed past me, shut the door, and sank to the floor.

Her eyes widened even more. "I think your friend's hurt."

Clyde. The hit he had taken looked worse than mine. The energy the lizard guns fired was spreading across his chest. He was fading, winking in and out. I knelt beside him, swinging my hands back and forth across the glow that had eaten half his chest, afraid to touch it, and I cursed myself. I was

useless, an idiot that got his partner killed because he couldn't come up with anything better than a cavalry charge. No, worse than killed. Lost. Condemned to his real life. I knew enough about his original timeline to know why he didn't want to go back.

His eyes glittered in terror on some scene from his past I couldn't see. I tried to lift him to a sitting position, and my hands went through him.

"Come on," I begged him. "Try, partner." I could make out the worn planking beneath him now. I wanted to shake him, force him to try, but my fingers gripped air. He was almost nothing. "Clyde!" A shout that hurt, then a whisper, "Stay a little, dammit."

A grunt came from the shadows. For the first time I noticed the figure curled there, bound and gagged, a balding, chinless man in black who watched me with deeply calm eyes. The stolen goods. Mercy glared at him. "Shut up," she said.

Voices outside. The lizards were afraid of damaging the goods, but they would risk rushing us any minute. I thrust my hand into the ball of light that had been Clyde's head and squeezed. The wave of disrupted time leapt up my arm, knocked me backward. Pearls of light flew out and away, little Wells of pain and memory, each one a world, a minuscule scene that sparked upward and vanished. Mercy swore behind me.

"John?" Clyde's eyes were open. He looked haunted. A waxy sheen of sweat covered his skin, but the light had left. He was whole. I took a deep breath and helped him sit. He sat gazing at his hands, balling and unballing the fists. "Try to shake it off," I told him. "We don't have the time." Then I leaned close and whispered, "It never really happened." Our secret motto.

It seemed to help. He stood, still shaky, and I gestured to Shakespeare. "There's the goods. And this." I pointed to the dead lizard. "The lady here's been holding the fort for us."

I turned the corpse with my foot. The spray of oily scales across the lizard's cheeks made me shudder. Except for the reptilian alteration, he was human. He wore slick black coveralls from which a folded piece of paper peeked. I inched it out.

its a proven fact
shakespeare stops wars

No wonder everyone was after the Bard. "Someone's running an ad campaign," I told them.

Mercy had risen from her crouch. She glanced at the handbill and drew an identical one from her pocket. "They came flying up our Well one day. Our people traced them to their origin. That's how I knew what world to find him in." She jerked a thumb at the gagged playwright. "They're from your world."

"What?" said Clyde.

From our world. Advertisements thrown into the Well by someone with access to the basement room. I had a vision of Sanchez or Todd Gordon slipping into the unattended chamber, tossing in a handful of computer-printed fliers that fluttered away into a myriad parallel worlds with Jump technology, all willing to believe that the lack of a certain dead white male in their past was the cause of the war they inflicted on themselves in the present. Yet I couldn't imagine a motive. If one of our esteemed colleagues wanted to make trouble for Clyde and me, there were easier ways. Encouraging other worlds to steal from ours only created work for us. A little excitement.

What had I said to Sanchez? We like to Jump.

I should have figured it out then, but the shot I'd taken in front of the theater had slowed my brain.

I fingered the note. Something in the style of it bothered me. "Did it help?" I asked Mercy. She had moved away and sunk onto a stage-prop throne, rubbing her arms for warmth. The gun with which she had defended the door lay forgotten in her lap. "I suppose you dropped him off here and went back to your future to check. Did his writing keep your war from happening?"

"It was worse," she muttered. "The weapons were…different. More powerful. It's because he didn't write the plays he wrote in your past. Something changed. All he ever writes about here are—"

"Alks," said the Bard. I turned. Clyde had untied him and removed his gag. The man in black stood now, dusting himself with elegant, womanish flicks of his strong hands. It wasn't the first word I'd expected to hear from the golden tongue. It sounded like a duck burping.

"What did you say?"

"He said 'alks.'" Mercy scowled from her throne like a moody queen. "The alchimical carriages." She gestured out the window in the back wall of the alcove. A road curved around the bottom of the hill where London's tendrils stretched to encircle the theater, and along the road came a machine that was an unholy cross between a Model T and a bathtub. I recognized the putt-putt sound as the one I'd heard outside the inn. From the other direction came a second tin lizzy. Where they met on the narrow road, the drivers braked, stood up behind their wheels, and began to honk impossibly loud horns at each other. Tiny arms gesticulated. "Of course it's a primitive design," Mercy said. "They look different in the future. Surely you have them too."

"We—ah—don't invent them until the nineteenth century."

She wasn't listening. From the baseboard of the throne she pulled a handful of manuscripts. Stage plays. "Here...and here." A stack fell and skittered across the floor. "He's fascinated by the technology. He made us rename the theater." She dragged more of the thin, bound copies from behind the throne and chunked one over her shoulder. It hit me in the face. "He says he had this vision just after I brought him here. About alks flying to the moon some day. Now it's all he writes about. When I went to the future to check, his writings had changed our entire technology."

I glanced at the manuscript in my hand. Florid Elizabethan script proclaimed *A Midsummer Moon's Dream*. Mercy thrust another title at me. *Much Ado About Mars, A Comedy*. Below it lay *The Merchant of Venus*. "He's working on a new one now. Alk drivers reach the moon and fly on to the stars. What's it called, genius?"

Shakespeare had moved quietly to my side. The smell off him was bearable only because I'd grown up on a farm. Like cows after a rain. In the golden age of Elizabeth, they hadn't discovered baths yet. "*The Tempest Star*," he replied to Mercy's question. The dignity in his voice made Clyde look up from the pile of ropes and costumes he was examining. We exchanged glances. A world that invented the combustion engine in the 1500's, has time travel, and yet considers space travel a wild fantasy. Mercy's world was wacky, but we'd been in crazier parallels before.

"Man will never fly to the moon," Mercy told Shakespeare. He drew himself up. "Witched am I perhap, woman, by these machines, yet my vision is greater than thy pewling." Secretly I agreed.

"Put a sock in it."

"Thou didst bring me here—"

"Well, you're going home now."

"Thou liar! Wouldst bear me to some other strange world!" The thick hands clenched and unclenched.

"Calm down," I told him.

"Belike you, sir, are a man of honor." Though I stood a head above him, the strength of Shakespeare's gaze made me feel small. He looked me straight in the eyes. I began to like him. "I would go home now, to New Place. To mine own London. To...." Maybe words failed him. He swallowed. "Do swear you that I shall be brought thither."

"Believe it, pal."

He took a deep breath. "You have said well."

"John, I have an idea." Clyde found a long hemp rope and draped it over the transom above the back window. I looked down. The hill on which the theater sat ended sharply at the building's back. Between the height of the window and the descending slope, it was quite a drop. Clyde winked at Shakespeare. "Ever rappelled?"

Mercy pocketed her gun and hoisted herself to the sill. "Anything to get us out of here. Show me." Shakespeare watched Clyde loop the rope about her leg and shoulder. His face went dark.

"I cannot," he said.

"Afraid of heights?"

"Not so. I've been a god." He gestured up at a small manhole in the top of the alcove and the winch that hung there, then glared again out the window. "Yet this is madness."

Clyde shrugged. "We can't call the Well up in a small space like this. It'd kill us all. We have to get out there."

I stared up at the winch. "They lower gods to the stage with that or what?"

"Or ghosts. Gods and ghosts do fly. Witches crawl 'neath the earth." With his toe Shakespeare nudged the iron grip of a trap door.

A trap door. A tunnel beneath the stage, so that all those Elizabethan ghosts could appear out of thin air. Outside, heavy boots thudded onto the stage. "Clyde, think you could work this winch?" He saw what I was getting at and grinned. He left Mercy at the window and began to sort the ropes and pulleys that controlled the flying mechanism. I wrenched open the trap door. Dank air struck me.

"Up you go, god," Clyde ordered Shakespeare. "They won't shoot you. I just hope you're as good at diversions as your rep." The Bard understood. He scurried up the ladder and slipped into the leather harness connected to the winch. Clyde gave me the go sign. "You're crazy, you know," he told me.

"I just hope my horse is still there."

Then I was down through the trap door. The packed earth beneath the alcove was dry. Light fell through cracks in the stage, striping the low tunnel. I had to bend low as I moved, running the back of my hand across the underside of the planks until I found the ring of the trap door leading onto the stage. Through the cracks, I could see the soles of the lizards' boots tangling with their darting shadows, turning toward the alcove, away from me. I heard a creak, and shouts arose. The god they had come for was descending. Their heads would be up. Shakespeare's voice sounded:

"Arm, arm and out!

There is nor flying hence, nor tarrying here.

I 'gin to be aweary of the sun,

and wish the estate o' the world were now undone.

Ring the alarum-bell! Blow, wind! come, wrack!

At least we'll die with harness on our back! Alarum!"

It was my cue. I scrambled to the stage. The lizards had their backs to me, shifting, waiting for Shakespeare to drop within reach, but he had begun to swing by pushing off from the wall. A lizard turned and saw me. "A horse!" came the Bard's wild voice from above. "My kingdom for a horse!"

My dray stood nibbling grass, its back level with the stage. I swung onto it, swimming for the reins. Shots sizzled past. Shakespeare swung again, half-fell at the edge of the stage, flicked the harness off, and leapt on behind me. I couldn't have done it better myself.

In another world, Shakespeare goes to Hollywood and becomes a stuntman.

We burst through the entrance in time to see Mercy and Clyde dart from behind the theater. Clyde was madly working his belt controls to signal the techs. The Well cone popped into view, and they Jumped in. We had seconds. "Hold on!" I yelled to Shakespeare and aimed the horse straight for the point of the cone. Distortion swallowed us—

—and the horse rolled, kicked, and trotted away to try out the columbine growing in the shade of the theater. A different theater, larger and less weatherbeaten. Mercy helped me to my feet.

"It's your London," Clyde told Shakespeare. "Our London."

The Bard stood. He still had the Well in his eyes, a ghost of fear that made him blink

stupidly. The fall had tousled his hair. Strands lay plastered with sweat across his bald spot. I felt sorry for him.

"You can find your way home from here, can't you?" I said. He nodded and waved a finger vaguely in the direction of the Thames. I wanted to say something to help him. "No alks," I commented. He grimaced. "I guess it takes getting used to, all this switching. The Well sort of does things to you." He still didn't reply. "At least you know more now than when you left."

He looked at me, and then his gaze wandered to the Well shimmering beside us. "I know we are such stuff as dreams are made on." He extended a finger into the Well cone, watched it disappear up to the knuckle. As he pulled it out, the cone wavered and disappeared. "I'm free to leave?" he asked. I nodded. I wanted to shake his hand, but it seemed too trivial a gesture. He started to go, then turned and bowed to me and Clyde, ignoring Mercy. "Farewell," he said. "And thanks."

I watched him make his way down the hill for a long time before I turned back. Clyde and Mercy had walked a few feet away. Clyde whispered earnestly to her. With a look of disgust, she handed him the crumpled Shakespeare advertisement, and I watched him stuff it into his pocket.

Something flipped over in my mind.

I must have looked like I'd been kicked. He started when he saw me staring.

"You...." I stepped to him and grabbed the handbill from his pocket. He jerked back as though he thought I would hit him. "You printed these up and threw them down the Well!"

"I didn't know it'd have any effect. It was an experiment."

"Why, goddammit?"

"Because nothing ever happens, John! We sit there filing reports and now and then we Jump—we put our lives on the line and save the world—and all we get are funny looks because of what we are. We go back and file another report and we wait. I wanted to make things happen. I want a reason for being there—"

"You caused the China-Europe War!"

"It won't have happened when we go back. Wake up, John. The only thing that's real is what we do here in the past. The future is like...wax. None of it's real. Not for us. Even if it was, what do you care? It's not our world anyway."

I stared at him while he summoned the Well back with his belt controls. He didn't want to look at me. "We have to have something to hold onto," I said. He looked disgusted at my naiveté. There was always something wild about Clyde. He wanted action. I just never thought he'd go so far.

He finished his adjustments. "You coming?" he muttered, turned toward the materializing cone, and Jumped.

Mercy watched me with pity. "You're both stolen goods, aren't you?" she said.

It didn't matter if she knew. "I was stolen from my own world," I told her. "I never knew why. It wasn't as though I was famous or anything." I thought again of the old apartment in L.A., the kid from Iowa dreaming of being a movie star and only making it to stuntman, until the strange man with antennas in his hand appeared at my door one night, grabbed my arm, and my whole world crumbled. I thought of him as my recruiter because what he did led me to be a chronocop, but he had had nothing to do with them. Why he had wanted to steal me remained a mystery to me. "The chronocops recovered me, and I told them I didn't want to go back. My life in my original world wasn't going anywhere. Not as far as I knew. Something similar happened to Clyde. He had good reasons for not wanting to go back to his life. So they trained us to do this, gave us jobs as chronocops. We're good at it, I guess. We don't develop the psychoses others do when they Jump too much, and they hate us for that. It's just that...it really isn't our world. Sometimes you get to feeling nothing's real at all." Like Clyde had.

"What happens to me now?"

"You're under arrest."

I took her arm, Jumped, and for the third time that day felt the void slide past, the nothingness of a million worlds clawing to get in. We landed on our feet in the control chamber. Clyde had called officers to take away Mercy. Lieutenant Sanchez hovered beside them as they snapped on the handcuffs. "You kill all the Indians?" he said.

"How's the Cube holding up?" I asked him.

"The what?"

"The war's gone, John," Clyde told me. "I already checked."

Sanchez turned to leave and threw the Shakespeare file over his shoulder at me. I caught it half-open. "The cowboys win," he said.

"No shots fired," I told his back.

The guard tugged at Mercy's arm, but I stopped him. She would have a hard sentence before being sent back: a year in isolation, no visitors, to minimize her influence on our world. "You know," I told her, "they'd give you amnesty if you decided to stay and become a chronocop."

She shook her head. "I have to go back. Try to change what Shakespeare didn't. But thanks anyway, Mr.—"

"Wayne."

She smiled. "You looked familiar. We have one of you, too." The guard led her away.

One of you, too. Somewhere, encrypted in the databanks, is a file on my future, a future the man with the antenna hands, for his own unfathomable reasons, had wanted to prevent. I would never see that file. I would never know if the future he cut short was good or bad. I'd stumbled across Clyde's file once, and it had been enough to scare me away from looking at my own. If the partner who'd stood beside me and saved my life ten times over could become a bank robber and murderer, who knows what I would have been? Even if it's against the law to drag souls across worlds and deposit them somewhere else, I was glad someone had done it with us. Screw the law.

The file on Shakespeare had fallen open to a photo of his grave, some dreary cathedral in England. I studied the inscription: *Cursed be he that moves my bones.* I could feel Clyde watching me. "What are you looking at, Barrow?" I said. He shrugged and looked away. He was afraid I was going to tell Sanchez about the handbills, but what did it matter? It was already a non-event. Just like he said. Nothing ever happens.

"Don't worry," I told him. "It's our little secret."

-dp-

THE LAUNCH

He was all of six
when he rode a 25 cent
rocket to the stars.

Now, twelve
decades later, he gazes up
at the first starship

as it sets sail
into blue sky morning, and
the night beyond,

collar turned up
against the cold, the sand
beneath his shoes

the recycled bones
of ancient stars; mankind's
oldest launch pad.

—G.O. Clark

THE WAY TO HEAVEN

by Jo-Ann Lamon Reccoppa

I sit on the front steps, and my eyes stray to my daughter, Jessie, playing on the skeletal remains of our discarded living room sofa.

I wonder, could I kill her?

The sofa burned three nights ago, when Jessie accidentally knocked over a candle. I thought the house would go up, but we were lucky. I managed to beat out the flames with my hands and drag the sofa out to the curb, as though the Public Works truck would come by to collect it in the morning. Jessie felt awful about it and cried so hard that I wondered if she would make herself sick. At times she can be too sensitive for her own good, though she has toughened up plenty lately.

She is a lovely child with long, silky hair—still pretty, though much of it has fallen out. She plays in the deep, chalky dust no matter how often I tell her not to. Her face is always dirty, and, though I try to keep her squeaky clean, such niceties don't seem to matter much anymore. I wash and rewash her with our supply of contaminated water. It's all we have left. I wonder if I am doing wrong or doing right.

The honeysuckle and lilac bushes have withered, and the front yard no longer smells as sweet as cotton candy. It once did—just as there were once bees buzzing in the roses, boys playing stick ball in the street, and giggling girls running carefree through the sprinklers on lazy, hot summer afternoons.

We have a roof over our heads and we are grateful for that. The initial blast shook our house all the way down to the foundation. Fortunately, it held. Most of our neighbors weren't so lucky. Their homes crumbled like sheet rock. The entire block looks like a scene from one of those megabucks, Irwin Allen disaster movies from the '70s.

"Be careful, Jess," I call out, and she glances over her shoulder to give me a smile as she precariously balances her slender

body on the arm of the sofa. I suppose she's pretending she's walking a tightrope, or maybe scaling the world's highest peak. You never know with Jessie.

She jumps down and heads toward the curb. Jessie stops and looks both ways first before crossing the street, makes a bit of a dramatic show of it, though there's no reason to do so. A car hasn't passed by for over a month now, as Jessie very well knows. The elaborate gesture, I assume, is her own private joke. It's actually very funny.

She strolls up the path and crosses the driveway of the house directly across the street. The Franklins have dug out a deep hole near their side gate. Jessie leans over and peeks in, curious, as the family lowers their youngest child into her final resting place. Jessie doesn't even shed a tear. She just wants to see.

They had been best friends, she and Debbie, until this morning. They had swum together in plastic pools wearing nothing but diapers. They went trick or treating together, watched Big Bird together, and started kindergarten together, while Susan Franklin and I stood on the sidewalk, smiling bravely to hide our tears on their first day of school. They colored in their coloring books with broken Crayolas, some with teeth marks in them if the shade of Sky Blue looked particularly appetizing. They had reached the age of seven side by side, and were closer than conjoined twins.

And then Debbie Franklin died.

Jessie doesn't seem affected by her passing. She accepts it, the same way she accepts the lack of food and clean water, and the hideous eruptions on her delicate, pale skin. Though an impressionable child, she has always accepted life for what it is. Jessie has come to terms with the way things are. She knows the score. All the kids on the block know the score—the same way they know

there is no Santa Claus, no Tooth Fairy, and no Easter Bunny. Word travels fast in the seven-year-old set.

"Jessie!" I call out, needing her comforting presence beside me. "Time to come home now!"

She walks to the curb, and, sure enough, she stops and cautiously looks both ways once again before crossing the street.

"What's up?" she asks, seating herself beside me on the middle step. Her voice sounds upbeat, lighthearted, but deep down she is miserable and in a great deal of pain. I know an act when I see one.

Her appearance alone is a good indication that she is not feeling well. Though the light is poor, the dark smudges beneath her hollow eyes are unmistakable. Still, she tries her best to keep her spirits up. She is valiant, my daughter. More brave than I will ever be.

"I want you to understand, honey," I explain gently. "Debbie was a very sick little girl. Her parents couldn't stand to see her suffer anymore. They loved her so much that they sent her to live with God."

"There's no fallout in heaven," Jessie recites by rote. "Everything's perfect in heaven and nobody ever gets sick."

"That's right," I agree, giving her a small hug.

"Are you gonna send me to live with God too, Mommy?" she asks.

I study her small, serious face and notice an oozing wound that has previously escaped my detection. When did that one erupt? I wonder. When will this nightmare end?

"I don't know, baby," I tell her truthfully. My heart breaks to consider it, but consider it I must. This is my daughter, my only child, and I watch, day after day, as her beautiful body deteriorates from the radiation that rips her apart from the inside out.

"Mr. and Mrs. Franklin did it to Debbie," she says in that queer, matter-of-fact voice of hers. "Karen Ann down the block had to do it to her brother. I heard old lady Becker did it to Mr. Becker with a steak knife. Debbie said Mrs. Becker cried so hard, that she threw up all over Mr. Becker's body! Of course, Debbie's dead now…."

Jessie's pixie face has a wistful, melancholy look. She hugs me, and the face upturned to mine smiles sweetly. Her expression changes abruptly as her tongue explores the inside her mouth. Finally, she spits a tooth into the palm of her hand.

"That's the fourth one this week!" she declares triumphantly, as though this is a rare accomplishment that only she can master—a regular gold medal winner in the post-apocalyptic Olympics.

"Honey, don't feel too bad," I tell her.

"I don't, Mommy," she says. "I'm the champ of the block at losing teeth! They're almost all gone now. Debbie still had six when she went to live with God."

We watch as the Franklins fill in Debbie's grave. The terrible, final thumps as clods of dirt hit the child's shrouded body will stay with me forever.

A spacecraft silently hovers overhead, as though in attendance at the makeshift funeral. The huge ship is as long as our street and as gray as the sky. Its odd, triangular appearance reminds me of boring days in Geometry class about a thousand years ago, when I was still in high school and there was such a thing as a future. The awful craft blocks out what little sun has managed to filter through the heavy, gritty air. Even in death they come to mock us.

The blasts have no effect on the aliens. Rather, they thrive on the radiation, as though it were vitamin rich, while our poor bodies wither away like my fragrant lilacs.

"I wish those ugly old aliens would go back to their stupid old planet and leave us alone!" Jessie says, stunning me with the sudden intensity of her feelings.

"Me too, baby," I whisper, mentally telling myself it's too late, it doesn't really matter anymore because the damage is done. Those invading abominations from far-off have done good work for themselves. They have raped our world and pillaged our resources and created a perfect environment for their hideous race—these faceless, nameless creatures. They have killed off the entire planet to duplicate their own obscene habitat.

"Do you think God loves them too?" Jessie asks out of the blue. "Do you think they send their kids to heaven to live with God?"

I see the panic in her eyes and I panic myself. I will not have my daughter dreading heaven when she looks there for eternal peace. I damn Jessie's Sunday School teacher for telling the children that God has created all things and loves all of his creations.

"No!" I tell her quickly, and the undeniable severity in my voice makes my daughter wince. "God hates them all! He won't allow them into heaven. No way! Heaven's only for us, honey. No aliens allowed!"

Jessie grins, temporarily pacified. Across the road, the Franklins finish tamping the dirt on Debbie's grave and trudge back inside their shell of a house. The alien ship, impartial to human suffering, slips silently away. Jessie watches its departure with an almost apathetic interest, then turns and vomits into the dead grass beside the steps. She looks up at me with those haunted brown eyes and slumps sideways, her sagging body supported by the wrought-iron railing. She's coming to the end, I know. She only has a few days left, surely no longer. I can't stand to see her suffer anymore.

I leave her side and enter the house. In the bathroom, I search for the pills prescribed for my allergies two short months ago. I find them in the medicine cabinet, along with codeine based painkillers. On another shelf is a bottle of pills from the time I threw out my back, though these have long since expired. I take them anyway, and stop in the kitchen to fill a tumbler with water from the plastic jug.

I wish for someone to lean on, someone to shoulder the burden, but there is only me. My husband was at work when the first blast hit, close to ground zero, I'm fairly certain. He is a lucky man to get off so easy. I don't think he would be capable of doing what I have to do. He doted on Jessie—like most fathers do with their daughters. It would kill him to do what must be done, but then, he would die anyway. Like I will. Like we all will in the next few weeks.

I must do this alone. Alone, I have come to realize, is the most terrifying word in the English language.

I hope, as I return to my daughter's side on the steps, that I can rouse her enough to take the pills, and that her sensitive stomach has quieted enough so that the pills will stay down long enough to do the job.

Jessie's eyes roll back in her head and her little body convulses—arms flailing and legs kicking out at the dusty air. I must wait until the convulsions stop and she is resting easier.

I pet her head, like I used to when she was a baby, and sing a lullaby. My voice cracks, I get the words wrong, and yet I know that the sound is still soothing and strangely comforting to a child's ears.

I hope Jessie's throat hasn't closed up so tight that she can't swallow liquids, and that there is enough room for the pills and capsules to slide down without too much trouble.

I don't want to be like old lady Becker who lives down the block.

I don't think I can use a steak knife.

CLOAK MEN

Has he ever come
in the middle of the night
to take you to his land
of shadows and pain
and evil mirth spilling
from the jaws of demons?

Have you seen him
hovering over a sick bed,
a noxious presence that
all could perceive
yet none would declare?

Have you worn
the cloak yourself?
Have you knelt in penitence
before a god in whom
you seldom believe
and performed insane
and obsequious rituals
to appease the rage
in his holiness?

Have you held your head
at a certain angle?
Have you laughed
when there was nothing
to laugh about?
Have you bedded down
with hideous incarnations
whose treacherous craft
you hope to snare?
Have you watched
1000 atrocities committed
in the cold light of reason?

—Bruce Boston

I Gave At The Orifice is a chapbook of some of Mark McLaughlin's **weirdest stories.** Here you will find an **evil sculpture and a freaky catman in a rubber suit** ... a society of underground **fungus-eaters** ... a tentacled, **koala-nosed monstrosity** ... a weirdo driving around in a **whispering car** that runs off his sweat ... a waspy secretary, worshipped by the **secret world** inside her computer ... and **more.**

$3.50 postage paid Mail check or money order to:

Eraserhead Press
16664 E. Trevino Drive
Fountain Hills, AZ 85268

www.eraserheadpress.cjb.net

"McLaughlin is HOT!" – Novelist Simon Clark

ZOM BEE MOO VEE & Other Freaky Shows by Mark McLaughlin is a chapbook of stories about movies and TV programs that you've never seen. They do not exist. There is no foreign movie called **Oh, But You Will.** No bedroom comedy called **Grandmama's Naughty Perfume.** And there has never, ever been a horror film called ZOM BEE MOO VEE. **UNTIL NOW...**

"Pure twisted delight! ... ZOM BEE MOO VEE is one hell of a show!" – Don D'Auria

"McLaughlin's tales are laugh-out-loud assaults on consensus reality." – Paul Di Filippo, Asimov's SF

$5.99 All copies signed by author.

Mail check or money order to:

Fairwood Press
5203 Quincy Ave. SE • Auburn, WA 98092

www.fairwoodpress.com

Stone Dragon Press

is accepting novel-length work and short story collections.

Stone Dragon is a small but lively publishing house in St. Paul, Minnesota. *We use printing-on-demand to return control of the material to the creators*—our authors can write to their vision in their voice. You can say what you need to say the way you need to say it and not worry about your sales numbers.

Our authors are not assembly-line workers in an entertainment factory. We work closely with them and help them say what they mean to say, not what the Marketing Department says they ought to say or any other "Flavor of the Week" commandment about content.

Get the 100% pharmaceutically-pure dope on Stone Dragon at
    www.StoneDragonPress.com
or write us at
    2402 University Ave W #504
    St. Paul MN 55114-1701

VIRTUAL EMPATHY

by Connie Wilkins

A wall of heat hit me just inside the door. Outside, the winter air was clear and sharp, but trapped sunlight cooked row upon row of video tapes and spread the pungent tang of hot plastic.

Ian was with a customer. My foggy glasses fuzzed their shapes, but I could hear a female voice. "What great windows! You could be growing lettuce and herbs in here." If I took enough time defogging, would she take her rentals and leave?

"Here's the man now, hardly late enough to mention," Ian said. "How about it, Kit, can you grow us some virtual salad?"

He was edgy. I don't make much effort to block out Ian's emotions; he keeps them pretty much to himself. But that dumb remark and his tone of voice broadcast serious tension. Whatever was going on, I wanted out.

"Virtual coleslaw. I'll get right on it." I started toward the lab. My mornings are supposed to be free of customer hassles.

"Uh, wait, Kit, I have a job for you." He kept his eyes on the woman so he wouldn't have to face me. "This is Marty Ritter, from Hampshire County Hospice."

She started to extend her hand, then diverted it to the counter, perceptive enough to catch my slight, involuntary recoil. I don't much care for being touched.

"Hi, Kit, we really appreciate the help you guys are offering."

My startled expression was wasted on Ian.

"Right, Kit, I've agreed to donate some time on the virtual system and some customizing by you," he explained, still averting his eyes. "It'll have to be a house call, of course."

Of course. No wonder he couldn't face me. Giving away virtual time was his option, even if a few free movie rentals might do as much good. But to send *me*, to expect me to work with someone who was dying, and who *knew* it....No way would I

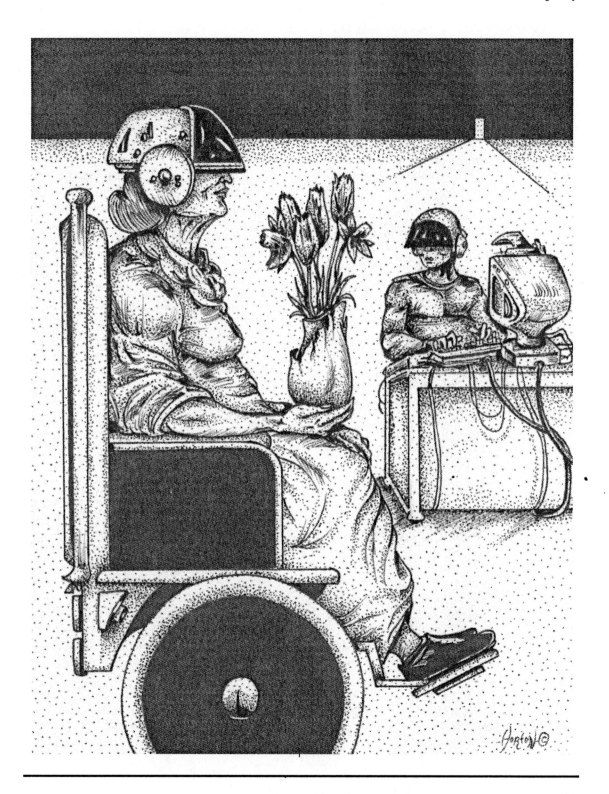

open up enough to make the customizing equipment work. He knows, suspects at least, how I do it, and he knows how it wears me down.

Even when he faced me, he wouldn't meet my glare. I got a grip and tried to sound rational.

"Why not take one of the studio releases? They're getting pretty good even without customizing." I nodded toward the shelves of virtual films, a small section growing fast in spite of the expense of the player rental.

"Yeah, right!" he said. "*Armageddon 8* or *Aliens: the Next Generation*. Or maybe something from the 'private stock' in the plain black cases?"

I eyed the customer warily. There are women's groups in the Valley who would picket or even trash the place if they knew about the "private stock," which is what really pays for the equipment. But she seemed cool with it, even amused.

Ian was still talking, and now he focused his pressure directly on me and zoomed right in. "Look, Kit, I wouldn't ask you if it wasn't important. The patient...."

"'Client,'" she interjected without rancor.

"Sorry, the *client* is an old professor of Heather's. They used to keep in touch until a couple of years ago, and when Heather heard she'd moved back here, she called. The professor didn't even remember her; she was sharp enough, but apologized for losing big chunks of memory. Heather was pretty torn up."

So Heather had talked him into this. Another reason, if I needed one, to avoid relationships.

There was no escape, but I gave it another try anyway. "The studios are virtualizing some real oldies. *Titanic* is coming out next week, and they're working on *Gone with the Wind*."

"Just go see her, Kit, try out some of your short tapes, see if she likes it. Nothing too extreme, maybe some of the scenic, outdoorsy stuff. Heather says she used to do a lot of hiking." He saw me formulating one more desperate gambit and cut me off. "Consider the upside for a change. You could try some far-out experimental moves, if she agrees. She's not going to worry about long-term side effects of electromagnetic fields, or addiction, or 'brainwashing,' or any of that. How can you pass it up?"

I could, but he wouldn't let me. He was my boss, and a pretty good guy, and nobody else would or could give me access to the technology I need.

"Okay, okay. When do we do it?"

"Right now, just for a test run. I've packed up most of the gear already."

Damn, he wasn't taking any chances.

In the van, with Marty Ritter, I tried to maintain total tech mode, but she made small talk. "Ian tells me you're a virtual film student at Hampshire College."

"Sort of. Part time." No way could I afford full tuition or keep up with enough courses for a degree, but no way could they have virtual film classes without guys like me.

She understood well enough. "I'm really sorry we can't pay you for your work. Ian seemed to think you might get some useful experience out of it."

"Ian pays me. Anyway, at Hampshire they teach that if people will pay to see your films, you're doing something wrong."

She laughed, and her plain, blunt features lit up with an inner warmth. She was all right. She was doing something that mattered to somebody; it was outside my experience, but I could appreciate it.

"Do you do much of this? Customizing, 'house calls,' as Ian puts it?" She seemed genuinely interested, but I kept my eyes on the road and picked my words carefully, hoping my face wasn't as red as it felt.

"Not much. It's pretty experimental, and the equipment rental is outrageous. People who can afford it, or who want it enough to shell out regardless, usually want to use it in private. I fit the headgear to them in the lab and then they take it home. When they screw it up trying to 'turn up the volume,' which isn't how it works, they pay extra to have me fix it."

"Pornography has always been at the cutting edge of technology," she said companionably.

"Mmmm." I groped for a change of topic. "Do you do much of this hospice stuff?" Then I blurted out more than I intended. "How can you stand it?"

She considered the question as though it were new to her. "I'm not sure how I stand it. I guess when there's just so much you can't do anything about, if you find something you can do, you don't turn away." Then she shook her head with a self-deprecating grimace. "Or maybe I'm just addicted to feeling needed."

I should have kept my mouth shut. Why make her doubt her own best impulses just because I couldn't measure up?

My relief when we finally arrived was profound.

I opened the back of the van. By the time I made a belated lurch toward the passenger door, Marty was already getting out. "Can you tell me anything about the…the client?" I asked. "Sometimes it helps to know some background."

"She can tell you most things you want to know. Don't expect her to be senile. She's had some memory loss, but in most ways her mind's as strong as it ever was, which is saying plenty." She picked up one of the smaller equipment cases and started toward the house, then paused at the foot of the steps. "Her name is Frances Kemble, and she's a retired drama professor and playwright. Some of her work was pretty controversial for its time." She leaned closer, not enough to invade my comfort zone, and lowered her voice. "Her husband died about ten years ago. She'll probably follow him in four to six months, maybe longer if she can work up some enthusiasm for staying alive."

She didn't look at me as she moved up onto the porch, but I got the message. I hoped they weren't expecting a hell of a lot from me.

I didn't notice much about the house until I was inside, scanning for electrical outlets and appliances that might emit interference. The living room was a little artsy and had some earthy-crunchy attitude. I could work with somebody who lived here.

"Where's the old lady now?" I asked absently, not noticing that Marty had gone into the kitchen.

"That's old *woman*, to you!" The voice was strong in spite of fault lines in its resonance. "Turn me around, will you?"

She had been sitting facing the window. I pulled the wheelchair gently around.

Her hair was white, her face grooved. Her eyes were sunken and intense, and once her fierce gaze gripped me. Nothing else about her appearance made any impression.

"I've heard something about this virtual reality," she said, "but I haven't kept up with new developments in the arts for some time. *Is* it art, would you say, or merely technology?"

"I don't feel any need to label it," I told her. "Let's try it out, and then you tell me, if it matters so much."

There was more humor than challenge in the deep eyes. "Most days I have to pretend things matter, but I think I'm actually interested now."

"Okay, here's how it goes." I unpacked the gear and started fitting it to her and to myself. "You're going to watch a kind of film inside this helmet. The images will appear to surround you, as though you were right in the middle of the scene. If it were interactive, you'd wear special gloves, but this time it's just some scenery I shot last fall in New Hampshire. I usually use it as a neutral topic for adjusting the equipment."

"You enjoy the outdoors, then?"

"To tell you the truth, I never even noticed that the leaves change color until I saw it through the camera's viewfinder."

She tried to shake her head at that, but I held the helmet steady. "While you're watching the film, little flexible probes will touch your head gently in various places; you'll hardly notice them. Very slight pulses of electrical current will stimulate different areas of your brain, enhancing the illusion of real experience. This is the experimental part, but I'll be monitoring it and adjusting the input for your specific configuration. If you aren't enjoying it, I'll know almost before you do and modify it or stop it altogether."

She eyed the keyboard beside me. "You mean you're going to play me like a musical instrument?"

"Close enough. Does that bother you?"

"Not at all. I pushed enough buttons in my day."

"Yeah, I heard you wrote plays. I'll have to look them up." I snapped her visor shut, then my own. I took a deep breath, pushed "play," and tentatively slid open the gate in my mind.

The shadow of my father's anger stood guard there, as always. Sometimes, not so often in recent years, I can't get past that point, past the terror of the first time I understood that I was intercepting his emotions, feeling the rage he aimed at me as though it were my own.

Usually, I can shift into professional mode and work my way around the barrier. I've learned to separate myself from the emotions I intercept, to keep a disinterested distance even as I pick up subtle nuances. Maybe I've learned that defense too well. I have trouble actually sharing feelings even on the rare occasions I might want to, but those are too few and far between to constitute a valid sample.

This time I concentrated on the image of my "client's" deep eyes and tuned in to her mood.

We progressed along a trail through the glow of autumn woods. Rushing water gleamed and sang through the trees to our right; every now and then a rock-rimmed pool appeared, dappled with sun and shade and accented by the scarlet of floating maple leaves. I felt her slight tension ease.

I pressed keys to activate groups of electrodes, monitoring her emotions. Acceptance flowed smoothly into serenity, pleasure, and then, sooner than I had expected, the full intensity of joy.

The trail swung closer to the river. The water flowed faster now, its rush rising to a roar as we neared a small waterfall. I held a finger poised over the audio control while I checked her responses for discomfort, but what I found was something unfamiliar, something I couldn't interpret. She was feeling too much, a strange blend of elation and pain. Worried, I opened to her more fully, loosening my hard-learned professional control. She seemed to be questioning, searching, for something, someone....

Her emotions surged into a recognition so ecstatic that the third presence was real to me, too, as she clung to him in the golden woods, and their flood of feeling engulfed me.

It was too intense, too private to be shared. I struggled to pull back, to close the gate, but even after I had wrenched my mind away, my hands shook and my vision blurred.

What was happening? That presence, so real to her, didn't come from my films and gadgetry. I had never imagined, in any version of reality, such a bond between two separate beings. An ache of loss shook me, a yearning for something I wasn't even sure existed.

I took off my helmet and watched for physical signs of distress. No way could I intrude again into her emotions.

When the film clicked to an end, I shut off the power and waited for some sign. Finally she lifted her hand to the visor with a slight tremor, and I gently removed the apparatus.

Her eyes were fixed on distance; as they gradually focused on me she reached out an unsteady hand to grip mine.

"How…did you do that?" Her faint whisper was frayed. My throat couldn't produce any sound at all.

"I remembered!" Her voice strengthened. "I found memories, some of them, the ones I needed most!" She searched inwardly again. "No…no…they're fading now…but at least I have a memory of the memory." She was still for a long moment, then went on, almost to herself. "So many times I thought, 'I will have this moment forever, hold on to it, never lose it, this joy, this closeness….'" Her voice broke, and I felt her effort to regain control.

Then those deep eyes looked searchingly into mine. I wondered whether she could see that I had no memories to lose. "It's hard on you, isn't it, painful, whatever it is that you do."

I nodded, still not able speak.

"I don't want to ask, but I can't help it. Could you do this again for me, soon? Even tomorrow?"

" I don't think…." I cleared my throat. Her disappointment flowed into me. "I don't think any of my other films would trigger the reaction we got today, but we can try to put something together. If you could tell me what kind of surroundings, atmosphere, even musical cues you think might work…."

"There are pictures," she broke in eagerly, "and letters, and journals. I go over and over them, struggling to truly remember, but I can never quite get there! It hurts so much I'd stopped trying." She looked away as though to shield me from her pain.

"I'll work up something, maybe a Ken Burns-type documentary. And we can always rerun the film we ran today."

"Are you sure it will be all right? For you?" Her compassion was a gentle touch in my mind. She must be a bit of an empath herself.

"No, but I can't not do it." I knew she understood. "I don't guarantee it will work again, but we have to try."

She smiled and echoed my awkward words. "If you 'can't not do it,' it must be art. Or maybe, in your case, magic. Whatever it is, thank you!"

I looked down, embarrassed by her gratitude, and saw that her clenched hands were shaking. When I looked up again, her eyes had closed and her smile faded.

"Marty?" There was a note of panic in my voice.

She was right there with a cup of something hot and a gentle touch on Frances' trembling fingers. When she turned and put a hand on my arm I didn't mind all that much.

"Can you wait a few minutes while I help Frances to bed?"

"Is she all right?"

"I'm just tired," Frances murmured. "Even joy can be tiring."

I wouldn't know, I thought as I packed up the helmets and console and cables. I didn't want to wait for Marty; I *absolutely* didn't want to come back here tomorrow.

When Marty rejoined me, I knew by the look on her face that I had no choice.

"How did you do that? Did you know what would happen? Can you really do it again?" There was a strained sort of awe in her voice that almost made me want to live up to it.

"I don't know what happened myself!"

"But you'll try?"

"Yeah, I'll try. Damn it, you were right about how you can't turn away. But I still don't know how I'll stand it."

She clearly wanted to say more, but just as clearly she could tell how close I was to the edge. We loaded the van and rode back to the video store in silence. By the time we got there, the tech side of my brain had begun to analyze the possibilities and plan some experimentation. It was a relief to have an emotion-neutral motive for getting involved.

It did work again. And again and again, not always, but often enough to show progress. There seemed to be some gradual improvement in memory even between sessions. The technology had therapeutic applications no one had considered. My own personal methods made progress a little easier and faster. I could envision working the process to a point where anyone with the technical knowledge could get results. And I could see all too clearly how such power over the mind could be corrupted.

I kept at it only for Frances Kemble's sake, even though at times I silently cursed her for making me care. The first time we evoked painful memories, I shut down the system, and then flinched at the rage in her eyes when she removed the helmet. "Don't ever do that! It's my life, and I want it, all of it!"

"All right!" I snapped back. "But I don't have to go there with you!" Once we'd both cooled off, we worked out a system where I could pull out if I needed to, and Marty, monitoring Frances' pulse and blood pressure, would have the final say on when to abort a session. It only happened once or twice.

With some reluctance, I let Frances persuade me to show her some of my less innocuous film work. Her reaction was analytic and occasionally, though she tried to hide it, amused. "Powerful imagery," she pronounced, "and some inspired juxtapositions. But I'm afraid I'm too weak on the context to entirely comprehend where you're going with it."

"'Going somewhere' is as antiquated as plot and linearity," I said, and we launched into one of our frequent arguments about art, technology, and the shifting interfaces between reality, virtuality, and truth. I sometimes thought that the intellectual combat did her more good than the memory work.

Not enough good, though. Marty took me into the kitchen one morning for coffee and fresh muffins, as she often did, but this time she stood looking out the window for a while in silence, absently stroking the potted herbs on the sill. The leaves released their savory essences into the sunlit air, but she didn't seem soothed by them.

"It won't be as long as we'd hoped, Kit. A few weeks at most."

The surge of grief that hit me might have been partly hers, or it might have been all mine. It didn't matter.

"Have I been wearing her out? I thought you said it would help...."

"Sometimes the mind keeps the body going longer than you'd think possible, but sometimes it isn't enough. None of it is your fault. You're giving her the fullness of her life, for as long as she can use it. That's the best any of us can do."

I wanted to ask how she could stand to go through this time after time, let herself care and lose friend after friend, but she was too fragile right now. Besides, I really didn't want to go there. Whenever either woman had brought up the possibility of my working with other hospice clients, I'd been noncommittal at best. Marty wanted me to confer with a doctor associated with the Hospice program who was very interested in what we were doing, but I had adamantly refused. There had been enough psychiatrists in my past.

I couldn't go through this again, no matter how much more I might learn. Damn it, virtuality was my escape, my alternative, better and brighter (or, if I chose, darker) than reality. I only put up with enough "real life" to keep mind and body marginally together and to get access to the technology that let me escape.

"Kit, are the memories real?" Marty had turned from the window, and I saw traces of tears on her face.

"As far as I can tell. But yeah, I could probably plant false ones if I wanted to. The whole process, messing around with the brain like this, is too damned dangerous. Leave VR to entertainment and let it go at that. There are uses for technology a hell of a lot worse than pornography and escapism."

I'd managed to jolt her out of her low mood. "The false memory business is already thriving without your gizmos," she said tartly. "It might be more valuable to develop ways of telling the true from the false."

"It could be done," I said, "with more test subjects...." Then I saw where she was going. "It's no use getting devious with me, Marty. I'll stick with Frances until...well, I'll go all the way with her. But that's it. No more. I have things to do, films to make." And reality to avoid.

I did go so far as to let Marty be a control subject for some research, comparing the two women's reactions. The first time we got really into it, she came out with a strange look on her face.

"Kit, if I had any money, I'd buy stock in you!" she said. "My memory is fine, but you...you magnify it, make it real, immediate. You could do so much, if you only would!"

"Of course he will," Frances said, with what passed for emphasis these days. Her strength was steadily fading, but she refused to acknowledge weakness. "And so will we, by having been in on it from the beginning. You're going to make me famous, Kit, in ways my plays never could."

What could I say to that? And she knew perfectly well the trap she had laid. But it wouldn't matter much longer.

I tried to fend off sorrow by filming things to give her pleasure—and planning how I would later twist the same images into visions dark enough to satisfy my mood. Spring flower shows at the local college greenhouses were bursting with bright satiny tulips and crisp daffodils; I brought her a bouquet to add scent to the visuals, but as she watched I envisioned teeth edging the fat red tulip petals and the daffodils' frilled trumpets elongating into obscene, writhing serpent-shapes, until everything melted into streams of green-black slime. It was only briefly satisfying.

I was with her at the end. And with us, I felt, because she felt him, was that third presence who had joined us on the virtual woodland trail.

When Marty arrived, I accepted her hug because she needed to give it. Then I left to find refuge in the life—or half-life—I had known before. It wasn't easy.

The day after the funeral, Marty called. "I hope you don't mind, Kit, but I want to tell you before the lawyer calls. I witnessed her will. She left the house to you. And some money, enough to get by. A grant for a fellow artist, she said, with no strings attached. She wanted to be sure you understood that part."

No strings. Right. I felt like a marionette when I called Marty a week later. "Okay, you've corrupted my art, technology, whatever. I'll do what it takes, use the tech force for good. Plug me into the program. Turn your doctors loose on me." Maybe "going somewhere" wasn't all that antiquated a concept. I might even pick up some memories along the way.

-dp-

UNSPOKEN

Small words—
distant sounds
a voice made
from no mouth

(a mind, held by
no head?)

oh radio show
exhale, speak
the only way
we can

all creatures
have voices

Unremembered—
machines do it
for us; it seems
natural now.

So too
their unspoken voices
silent throats
immobile lips

It's only static
a wave
a particle
(it sounds like voices)

Naw,
we're all alone.

—Denise Dumars

FAN LETTER

Dear sir,
I thought that you should know
That I'm your biggest fan.
You bridged my stages…
Child, teen, adult…
And still I love
Your work.

I read
About your exploits in
The papers, list your tours
In heart-stamped books
And link our names with
Arrows wreathed and carved
On trees.

I saw
You once, not close enough
To touch, but close enough
To touch your leavings.
Spent, rejected, peaceful
Cast-asides of
Power.

I've seen
Your lovers' faces in
Repose, the stress of life-
Times left behind to
Rot and breed new life,
The bastards of
Your love.

I know
Your groupies' lot, I've heard
The muffled moans and sighs
Of culmination,
And, dear Death, I want
A chance to share
Their fate.

—Marcie Tentchoff

THE ARTIFICE OF RESPIRATION

by Robert Subiaga, Jr.

Quentin flipped the switch and fluorescence banished the darkness, but not the emptiness. The medical examiner's laboratory was a tomb, after all, albeit a well-scrubbed and sanitized one. And Quentin immediately decided, for the first time ever, to forgo his usual pot of coffee. Caffeine would do nothing for this kind of lethargy.

"Quentin E. Devereaux, at your service," he called out mechanically, knowing only his own echo would reply. "Quentin E. Devereaux," he added in a voice softer, but hinting at more real emotion. "Q.E.D."

Quentin used his fingers to comb back the thin hair, blond enough to be near-white, that lay, flat and oily, on his oversized head. He lathered with specialized soap over the lab's stainless steel sink and scrubbed his hands until they were as raw as they were sterile, then donned protective goggles, latex gloves, and a disposable smock to protect him from the inevitable flecks of blood, of mucus, of flesh.

"The oldest adage in medicine is about pathologists," he said to the draped bodies. "We have all the answers. We're just always too late." The corpses said nothing in reply, even though this was approximately the four-thousandth time Quentin had repeated the joke. But then, perhaps these bodies had never heard it. Quentin never had repeat customers.

Quentin scowled. "You are entering the most fascinating sphere of police work—the world of forensic medicine," he said, trying his best, in vain, to sound like Jack Klugman on the old TV show, "Quincy." Quincy, who solved murder on a regular basis in the course of conducting his job; Quincy, who seemed so warm and lovable because everyone knew he did not merely doctor corpses. Quincy, everyone knew, cared.

Quentin had experienced only disappointed frowns thrown his way. They came most often when he went beyond stating he was a doctor to clarify his specialty. "Oh,"

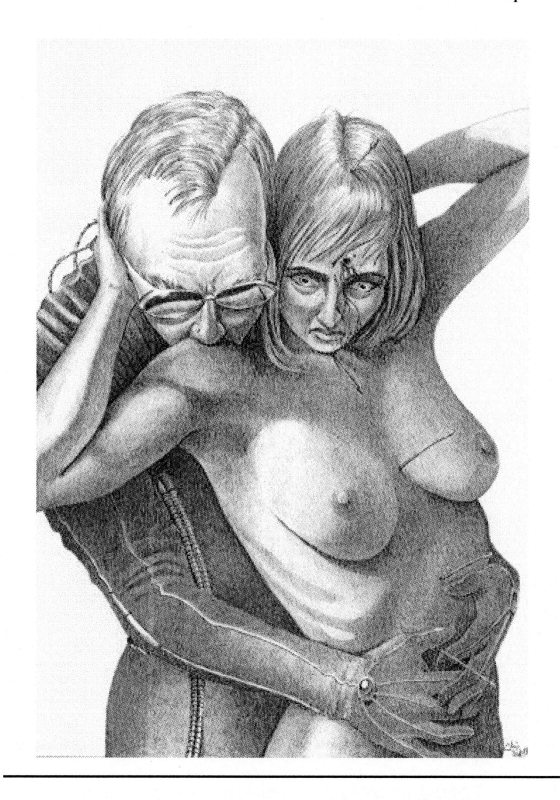

one debutante had said, staking out her claim to marrying-up at a party Quentin knew he never should have attended. "When you said you were a doctor I thought it meant that you *saved* lives."

At least she had been honest, if brutal. He always knew he was too fragile and timid in mental constitution to be a surgeon. Here, alone on the "graveyard" shift, where he had languished for sixteen years, Quentin's only companions were the car-loads of bodies belonging to tribes he called the Violently Killed. In a city like New York, such tribes beat their war-drums every night, and even those who thought they shunned such barbarism showed up to the party on Quentin's tables. The Auto Wrecks and the Drunken Accidents and Gang Wars and even the Innocent Bystanders. For too many years their anthropologist, Quentin had catalogued them all.

"I care too," Quentin said, wholly to himself.

No one knew.

They would. They would know soon, he kept telling himself; soon, they would know how much.

In his pre-med days, Quentin's ability to ace subjects as varied as philosophy, physics, or electrical engineering had been a boon; they impressed admissions committees. Yet his continuing drive to synthesize variant disciplines met with confusion at best. Outside of the particular field in which a term or concept was used, the response to its mention was a blank stare. With stacks of books and an occasional jerry-rigged device, Quentin worked alone.

He had the time. Why not? He had no other life.

Quentin laughed at himself; why not? The others at the morgue also laughed at him, the kind of silent, unconscious mockery they didn't even perceive, let alone thinking they meant him harm. If they thought of him at all, they might describe him as shy, and kind. His eunuch-like dedication to his job had found no more release than a half-dozen copies of risqué magazines and a couple unusual porno tapes hidden in his closet. Even Quentin's dementias were mild. His asceticism turned him quiet and disheveled in public, made him harmless and asexual in the minds of women he knew. They found him cute. Only when they saw him as impotent was it possible for him to seem attractive.

Quentin stared out over the still air of the morgue. As privileged as many of these still bodies might have been in life, compared to him, they had no such privileged existence now. It was up to him to save their still-living cousins, as they still moved, still breathed and fed and eliminated their wastes, all the while to participate in the rat-race and scarcely confront the fact that each would, one day, also become a corpse.

Quentin strode to the examining table. He ran his hand lightly over the sheet, and thus the contours of flesh beneath. The feel of well-formed breasts made him hard. Quentin's back stiffened and he started to pull away, trying to force down the memory of that thrill, and the shame it engendered.

For more than two decades he had been single-minded in his dedication to medical matters. "I've already frittered away so much of my life at this," he had told himself on thousands of nights before, in the same way as this night. "At this point, what's the harm in sacrificing just one evening more?"

He later was unable to remember if an intuitive shock really had coursed through him, filling him with dread even before he yanked back the linen cover and stared at the dead woman's face. The mind was tricky that way; even milliseconds after it thought or felt something, it reconstructed those thoughts and feelings with minor edits. But some things were more certain. The discrepancy between how he would have predicted his actions and feelings—and what really came. The fact that he did not cry, or rage, but knew only numbness, and a sudden dropping sensation in his stomach. A dissociated feeling, as if his mind had left his body.

Quentin of all people knew better; knew that that sensation, too, was a lie. But until the shock wore off, he was unable to act.

She was his own age. Her expression serene, her soft eyelids closed. The nostrils of her pert nose, sprinkled with freckles, so still. Her hair, golden and sparkling, barely covered the forehead whose ivory skin was so barely marred by a ragged-edged bullet hole. Yet it was neither the sight of her beauty nor her wound that made Quentin's chest tighten and his knees go so numb they started to buckle.

According to the standard conventions determining what constituted "having met" someone, Quentin had never met this dead young woman. Yet he had. Common wisdom also dictated that she was nothing but an object to him, a fantasy image fit for vicarious gratification. Yet to Quentin, a few moments of arousal had many times given way to hours of sad pondering.

Who was she, really, when he sought more than a name but an essence? What did she like to eat? Did she like the warmth of a thick blanket under which to curl in a chill room, or would she rather doze on top of the linens, under a tropical moon? In which of these did she find joy? Fear? Hope?

Now all those issues needed to be phrased in the past tense.

Then again, she had always existed in the past tense for him, from the first moment he had beheld her in ninth grade chemistry. Years he had carried a secret longing for her, even following her to the local community college when a scholarship to the University of Chicago had been offered to him. Those four years he had avoided her, terrified of facing rejection, perhaps catching a glimpse of her once a month. Until, his libido dampening and the demands of academics mounting, he had started forgetting.

It was a face, a body, that Quentin thought deserved to grace slick magazine photos. And, as attested to by that which lay carefully stored in the left-bottom drawer of Quentin's desk at home, her likeness already had seen print. Maybe, Quentin thought, flushing, she was no more than a carved doll to him. Maybe he had never seen her as a person after all. Only the sharp pains between his ribs protested otherwise.

The chart read "Jane Doe." Quentin's jaw hardened. None of the names by which he knew her were adequate, yet they were all she had. He saw blue bruises of needle tracks in her arms, and only now noticed the hollow darkness under her eyes, but nothing else marred her skin. Whatever tragedies had befallen her, it seemed they were recent. The bullet wound was the luck of a bad draw, and Quentin had seen the results of enough of those.

He reached out to stroke the flesh he had never before touched and had always wanted to. Now he knew how others felt, pining for a loved one. No matter how much better someone might know a husband or a daughter or a friend, compared to how well Quentin knew her, it was never well enough. This differed from the emotions many might feel upon hearing of his discovery, but only as a variation upon the same theme.

Quentin also felt the desperation they would feel when they lost the first loved one for whom there might be time to be saved.

Six hours. Sweating, Quentin knew too much time had gone by for anything more than an expendable experiment. Gritting his teeth, he knew he had to try to make it more.

Quentin's hands moved deftly. He was adept now at working the scalpel through the minimum amount of flesh and muscle. Then came the placement of thin needles, both on her skin and through the hairline incisions.

The patterns in which he moved were particular and left no room for error. Though in concept not unlike the Eastern principles of *hara*, or *chakra*, or *chi*, such primitive conceptions were more a liability than a guide. One needed the correct stimulation of the whole organism, but only in the proper sequence of stimulation of the parts. Nor could a surface approach suffice; penetrating the skin to stimulate deep muscle and nerve and organs was even more vital than the skin-level stimulation.

Quentin glanced at his stopwatch. She had been dead for eight hours now. Time was running out. Already, invisible to the naked eye, at the cellular level, tissue was degrading. Unregulated enzymes, no longer participating in a closed and communal chemical loop, selfishly chewed each cell's important organelles. It was already too late to resuscitate her permanently; that opportunity had passed mere minutes after her original demise. But he could give her back a few, brief moments, as impoverished as her thought processes would be.

He shook his head violently, trying to dispel the mounting headache. It never bothered him before that this was an experiment, that even if it seemed useless, there was value, data to contribute to refinements in procedure that would make future procedures more than short-term. Clinically applicable.

Quentin quickly donned the jerry-rigged wetsuit, in whose rubber was embedded an array of sensors. The patterns in which both her body and all its parts needed stimulation were impossibly complex to simply store and run off a digital computer, even were it done on the state-of-the-art supercomputers. Realizing this truth, accepting it, had led directly to his breakthrough of using a living creature's own metabolism as a crude template.

Pneuma, the ancient Greeks had called the stuff of soul, using the same word as "breath." This *pneuma* was made of no matter in particular but an incompressible pattern; this *pneuma* was what they shared.

Needle electrodes against her nerves now stimulated tremors in corresponding muscle. The patterns would bear fruit if the process were painstakingly followed in all its length and tedium. Quentin let the current flow, examining him and then flowing into her, phased in certain peculiar, non-repeating sequences. Finally, as was necessary, the dynamics of the field began to exceed properties that could be explained by mere classical electromagnetic theory.

Quentin lost track of time; of course, when time was a physical property whose characteristics changed subtly in a quantum-coherent field, and they both now bathed in one. He forced himself out of the trance and looked at the clock. The night shift would be over in two hours. If she awoke now, they would have just enough time together to see if it worked.

Quentin disconnected himself from the apparatus and stepped back.

The five or more minutes necessary for the cumulative effect dragged, for him, into an eternity. Then, jerking, haltingly, her hand moved.

It was a slim, smooth hand, once tan but now overlaid with a white hue, like chalk dust. She lifted the linen. Then she sat up and stood before him. Naked as Eve.

For a moment, she seemed to comprehend. Her gaze focused on him, and her round lips, still red from the lipstick she had been wearing when shot, formed a puckering circle. Quentin's heart thudded painfully against his ribs, not knowing whether to hope she would speak. For months he had sought to perform a resurrection where the subject was obviously aware and could say so. But this was not a mere test subject, it was *her*, and it was a near-certainty that he had raised her from the dead for only a few moments. The sensation was the same as over the course of countless long-past afternoons, when Quentin had not known whether to hope for a chance at her attention or dread it.

Then, just as all the others' eyes had, hers turned dull. Quentin held out his hand. She took it, much too obediently.

Quentin's head swam. An hour left. An hour that would pass with agonizing slowness if he terminated the experiment now, as he had all the others. He had marched her around the room, gotten her to sit and stand, to turn her head and grasp objects, yet each act was in a stereotyped motion that gave Quentin no indication she was thinking independently in anything more than a minimal way. And a minimal way was not enough.

Not enough. Not when the promise of resurrection he could hand to the world came as all such elixirs did: with a price.

Some theorists had long since hypothesized that quantum events in the weird, seemingly mystical subatomic realm were necessary to explain Life, or Consciousness. These theorists had potent critics who pointed out that the physiochemical dynamics of cells and organs and brains, despite being microscopic, were still too large for quantum effects to matter.

The problem was, both camps were wrong. And that also meant, in ways to which they were blind, each camp was partially *right*.

"It's like a bridge," Quentin said, looking away himself. "Say the most of it has to be constructed of wood, because stone will collapse under its own weight. But say the footings still have to be made of stone. The stone is like the quantum effects—their proportion of the bridge is small, even if the bridge's footings are necessary. Meanwhile, standard physiology, with its non-linear dynamics, runs the vast majority of the show. It's a classic, non-symmetric, imbalanced synergism."

Quentin turned back to her. She pawed lightly at her suit, ineffectually. Quentin shook his head. What use was it, to go on talking? He could tell her the quantum proponents always had looked for too large a phenomenon, for quantum effects that could be seen across a whole cell, or even groups of cells. They didn't find any, of course,because they expected too much.

So no one but him ever would have pondered whether large-scale quantum effects that didn't exist presently could be amplified when the non-linear dynamics part of the synergy was failing, with an *externally* sourced quantum coherence that did bridge entire groups of cells before too much tissue became necrotic.

A miracle. But, in the end, still a physical phenomenon.

The vast majority of humanity believed in a "soul," clamored for proof of it, and stubbornly disregarded proof against it. "Well, I found it," Quentin mumbled. "The problem is, it's mortal. Just like a body, it gets messed up. Just like a body, when it's messed up badly enough, it dies."

He stroked her cold cheek and added, "Dies, and never comes back."

What would the people of the world say, facing verification that there was no definite afterlife and that all the lives lost in history had slipped into Void? Would people welcome the opportunity to live forever, in the company of loved ones already alive and maintained by science, if it meant confronting the truth that those dead and buried were truly no more? Would they adore Quentin, this new prophet? Or seethe with contempt at this heretic, this blasphemer who robbed them of their cherished beliefs?

"Could they accept me," Quentin asked her, "when I'm even finding it difficult, when I see you again, when having you here doesn't mean jack, when I just have to part with you again, still never knowing you this time either?"

He thought she shrugged, but meaningless spasms were something he'd seen with earlier subjects.

Quentin doubted he ever had possessed the willpower to fight the multitudes who would oppose this. The religious who viewed science as Evil yet picked-and-chose like they did with all science, using the technology without confronting the challenges to their own beliefs. New Age flakes who loved quantum phenomena only because they thought it supported magic, astrology, or bizarre quasi-Eastern mysticism. Academic philosophers and logicians who had built ivory towers on classical logic, algorithms, Mind as "no more than a computer," and stubbornly insisted quantum effects were no place to look.

None of them saw their fundamental similarities. All sought an *essence* to life, something removable from that of which it was made.

"Flesh," Quentin said.

The woman he had wanted to love so much, one who, in another life, he even might have been fortunate enough to love, ignored him. All she did was walk in a dull, stereotyped shuffle back-and-forth across a too-clean floor.

"Say my name," he implored her. "Say, Q.E.D."

Not knowing what she was doing, at least as far as Quentin could tell, she came to him. She walked to the cold, shiny examination table upon which Quentin sat, and she stood at his side as if at perfect military attention.

Choking back tears, Quentin looked away. But he could not resist, after a few moments, looking back. Her dilated pupils stared at him, and she leaned her head toward him, tipping it quizzically. Compelled, Quentin reached up to touch her cheek. It was still clammy, though a bit warmer than the sixty degrees of the laboratory. Without a quick enough resurrection procedure, her body was incapable of generating much of its own heat.

Still exploring and confused as a child, she did what he had dreamed of for countless summers, and touched her lips to his. They were cold.

Weeping freely now, Quentin stood and took her in his arms. They danced. No tune played, but then the sounds of music would only confound her. She simply matched his own motion, and he made sure to move slowly enough. As though moving in water, they slowly whirled and glided and dipped.

Quentin took her slim neck and pushed her lips to his. She barely responded, but did not pull away. He probed her mouth with his tongue, lacking in practice and operating on a decade-old memory. She tried to emulate him with even less success, twining her fingers in his hair and working her mouth fish-like, mechanical.

Quentin cupped a breast in his hand; it was too firm, almost like rigor mortis, though that was impossible in adipose tissue, and Quentin had to be careful not to disrupt the delicate electrode needles emanating like porcupine quills from various parts of her body. Her nipples, of course stiff, were chill to his tongued kisses.

Quentin forced his hands to make circles over the firmness of her stomach, the indention of her navel, the soft hair between her thighs. He moved between them, his cock painfully hard. Yet he could never enter her, could not remove the sensor-imbedded wetsuit without her dying, as much as she struggled to tighten her legs around him as if desperate for the feeling.

Quentin led the pale form back to her table. She followed, still obedient.

He stroked her hair ever so gently as he delayed the lethal injection of tetrodotoxin he used to end each experiment a little prematurely, to be sure the subject didn't die in pain. Even with the aid of Quentin's resurrection techniques, her vitality began to ebb, and she laid down.

What was the use? Quentin thought as he twirled the now-hated syringe between his fingers. What was the use? Even with the aid of his techniques, death could not be forestalled forever. A horrendous accident could always disrupt a body's matter beyond the hope of even an advanced resuscitation setup. All Quentin had done was prolong life, and with it intensified the disappointment at its end.

What was the use? Quentin thought as he watched her eyes cloud over, now certain that these few brief moments he had given her were irrelevant at best, or a curse at worst.

Not bothering to remove the wetsuit, Quentin reversed the syringe and plunged it into his own heart.

He never felt the grasp on his shoulder of a hand, fighting from beneath a shroud, trying to stop him. He never heard her weeping voice, nearly incapable of speech but grateful for one more moment to feel and think and try, struggle to beg him, "No."

THE CLASSIC HORROR FILM: OF GERMANY AND THE SOUL

by Eric M. Heideman

I was born in June of 1953 and loved multimedia science fiction and fantasy before I could read. Horror took a bit longer to "take" with me. I looked into the *Classics Illustrated* comic book of Mary Shelley's *Frankenstein* as a small kid and it creeped me out. Then around 1960, when I was, like, seven, I saw a theatrical preview for the U.S. release of Hammer Studios' *The Mummy* (1959), with this imposing human figure (Christopher Lee), completely wrapped in rags, breaking a window open to strangle a guy, and carrying an unconscious woman into a swamp. That inspired the most vivid nightmare of my life. By 1963, when I was ten, I'd become a devoted builder of Aurora plastic models of knights in armor. That September I saw a comic book ad for Aurora's model of The Mummy, part of their Universal Studios classic monster series, and I just had to have it. That led, of course, to Aurora's Dracula, The Wolf Man, The Phantom of the Opera, King Kong, "Dr.

Jekyll as Mr. Hyde," and Frankenstein's Monster (called, as usual, "Frankenstein," the Monster and the Monster's maker bound together in the collective unconscious, two sides of the same Jekyll/Hyde coin).

Then, moment of moments, in January of 1964 I went to Payn's News for my fix of Silver Age Marvel and DC Comics, only to see a glossy magazine, *Famous Monsters of Filmland* #27, with a picture of a horned, scaly green-skinned Cyclops (from *The Seventh Voyage of Sinbad*) and a screaming headline, "The New Year's New Fears." Another recruit for Monster Culture; another toaster oven for editor Forrest J. ("4E") Ackerman (1916-). 4E's pun-laden, information-rich articles made the monsters and their wonderful-sounding films into friends even before I saw them, and I quickly developed a lifelong curiosity about the literature that inspired those films (read *Frankenstein* in 1964, *Dracula* in '65), and about the actors, directors, and makeup artists who made those films.

My love of the Universal and RKO studio classics of the '30s and '40s continued at Gustavus Adolphus College in St. Peter, Minnesota, where my mates and I caught them in the dorm TV lounge on *Horror, Inc.,* midnight Saturday nights. I worked on the college Films Committee fall of '74, and for Hallowe'en I booked a triple feature of *Bride of Frankenstein, Cat People,* and *King Kong,* and got to enjoy (and see others enjoying) them on a big screen. But as for new stuff... *Deliverance* (1972) and *The Exorcist* (1973) scared the bejeebers out of me. After that, it got harder to find new horror films with the poignancy and humanity of the classics. Most of the new ones were plain disgusting. From time to time I got my hopes up—especially in 1981, when both *Wolfen* and *Ghost Story* came out. But mostly it seemed that something precious had gone away, not to return, except in dreams.

Then came 1999, that nervous "fin de siecle" year before one changed to two and three nines to three zeros. I'm writing this in Spring 2000, less than a year after the release of two of the finest horror films ever made, *The Blair Witch Project* and *The Sixth Sense.* As I look back on these and at such recent flawed but interesting films as *Deep Blue Sea, Stir of Echoes, Sleepy Hollow,* and *the Ninth Gate,* as well the brilliant horror-related fantasies *Dogma, Being John Malkovich* and the darkly science fictional *The Matrix,* I again have my hopes up. I think that, this time, the classic horror film, mutating as always but clearly recognizable, entering freely and of its own will, has come back to stay for a while.

But what are retro grumps like me talking about when we celebrate the storytelling values of the classic horror film, and when we cast aspersions on films that use jillion-dollar special effects as a substitute for, rather than a servant to, those values? *The Sixth Sense* and *The Blair Witch Project* have been rightly praised for their technical brilliance. *Blair Witch* directors Eduardo Sanchez and Daniel Myrick have been lionized for making a virtue of their minimal budget, leaving most of the scary parts off screen, allowing us to imagine them. *Sixth Sense* director M. Night Shyamalan is celebrated for his restrained, "mainstream" use of scary elements in a film dominated by heart and humanity. All true; but when some critics have suggested that *Blair Witch* and *Sixth Sense* were *introducing* subtlety to horror, those critics betray their ignorance of film history. *Blair Witch* and *Sixth Sense* are so good not because they are something completely new under (or out of) the sun, but because they represent a heartfelt return to form.

In 1943 publisher Edmund Speare persuaded cinema's premiere bogeyman, Boris Karloff (1887-1969), to edit an anthology of scary stories. Speare sent Karloff hundreds of worthy-candidate stories, from which Karloff selected fourteen. In his introduction to that book, *Tales of Terror,* Karloff speculated on the origin of scary stories.

> Are you afraid of the dark? You know perfectly well that you are, and you may as well admit it. You come by it honestly. Imagine the sensations of that ancestor of ours who was the first to fall from his treetop, stumbling around in the abysmal gloom of those primeval jungles peopled by heaven knows what, all waiting to pop out at him from every shadow. And when, or if, he managed to scramble back up to his tree to safety...he began inventing all the ghosts and demons

he might have seen but never did; and it is those which delight and terrify us today.

Narratives that included elements of horror and terror were present in literature from its beginnings. The 18th century gothic novel, which began with Horace Walpole's *The Castle of Otranto* (1765) and perhaps reached its peak with the novels of Anne Radcliffe in the 1790s, featured exotic medieval settings and incidents that suggested the supernatural, only to explain the supernatural away as a hoax in their final chapters. Matthew Gregory Lewis broke free of this limitation in his frankly and luridly supernatural gothic novel, *The Monk* (1796).

In the early nineteenth century, E.T.A. Hoffman (1776-1822) wrote many creepy "Tales of Hoffman." About the same time, Jacob and Wilhelm Grimm solidified the German strain of terror by writing down and collecting many ghastly *marchen* (folk tales). In America of the 1830s and 1840s, as popular magazines began to flourish, those pioneers of the short story as a conscious art form, Nathaniel Hawthorne (1804-1864) and Edgar Allan Poe (1809-1849) often turned to morbid, eerie themes. Poe responded to charges that he was ripping off a uniquely German form when he wrote in the introduction to his first story collection, *Tales of the Grotesque and Arabesque* (1839) that "Terror is not of Germany, but of the soul."

Meanwhile, in the summer of 1816, while vacationing at Lake Geneva, Switzerland, the English poets Byron and Shelley, along with Byron's traveling companion and physician, Dr. John Polidori (1795-1821), and Shelley's eighteen-year-old lover, Mary Wollstonecraft Godwin (later Mary Wollstonecraft Shelley, 1797-1851) entertained one another with a collection of German ghost stories and challenged each other to a ghost story-writing contest. Byron wrote a fragment about a vampire. Polidori, inspired by that fragment, wrote the story "The Vampyre" (1820), modeling his brooding, romantic vampire on Byron himself. The story had huge influence. Vampire plays proliferated. Among many works of vampire fiction through the nineteenth century, James Malcolm Rymer's serialized novel, *Varney the Vampire, or The Feast of Blood* (1847) was especially popular.

And Mary, inspired by a wild late-night discussion about the artificial creation of human life, wrote the novel *Frankenstein, or The Modern Prometheus*. It was published in 1818, when she was still twenty, and has never gone out of print. Mary Shelley was the daughter of the leading feminist of her day, Mary Wollstonecraft (1759-1797) and the esteemed novelist and political philosopher, William Godwin (1756-1836). She grew up in a house full of books, listened in rapt attention as the leading intellectual and artistic lights of Europe came to visit (including Coleridge, who read the manuscript of "The Rime of the Ancient Mariner" to the Godwin household—a fantastic, horrific poem oft-quoted in *Frankenstein*). Despite her youth, Mary had, at eighteen, a vast background in literature, science, and current events, and she poured into her "ghost story" the potentials for creation and destruction in the burgeoning industrial revolution. She created a modern myth. (Indeed, it's doubtful if one person in 50 today knows who "Prometheus" is. Everybody knows "Frankenstein.") From *Frankenstein*, both science fiction and modern horror radiate in their different, though often parallel, directions. Almost immediately, Mary Shelley's myth branched to other media. The first of several stage adaptations, *Presumption: or, The Fate of Frankenstein*, premiered in 1823. She liked it.

The British ghost story, too, flourished through the nineteenth and early twentieth centuries, in the hands of such writers as Dickens; Irishman J.S. LeFanu (1814-1873), whose lesbian vampire novella, "Carmilla" (1872) has been oft-filmed; M.R. James (1862-1936), one of whose low-key supernatural tales inspired the classic film *Curse of the Demon* (1957); and Arthur Machen and Algernon Blackwood, whose tales of cosmic horror would influence America's H.P. Lovecraft.

Great Britain in the late nineteenth century saw the publication of American transplant Henry James' (1843-1916) keystone psychological ghost novella, *The Turn of the Screw* (1898—faithfully filmed as *The Innocents,* 1961), in which we're never sure whether the two children in the governess-narrator's care are possessed by evil ghosts, or whether the governess is simply insane. Century's end also saw the creation of three horror archetypes in Robert Louis Stevenson's (1850-1894) *Strange Case of Dr. Jekyll and Mr. Hyde* (1886), Oscar Wilde's (1854-1900) *The Picture of Dorian Gray* (1891), and Bram Stoker's (1847-1912) *Dracula* (1897). *Jekyll & Hyde*, like *Frankenstein*, quickly generated stage adaptations.

Dr. Jekyll and Mr. Hyde and *The Picture of Dorian Gray* are both tales of *Doppelgangers* (German for doubles. *Doppelgangers* have long been a subject of fantastic fiction, including Poe's "William Wilson.") Dr. Jekyll was a prim, virtuous, Victorian gentleman who took a chemical potion that let him explore his repressed darker side. Dorian Gray made what amounted to a demonic bargain that kept his face young and innocent while his oil portrait grew horrible with the image of his sins. David J. Skal has pointed out that film adaptations of these parallel stories have often traded elements, making,

for example, Mr. Hyde a sexual libertine like Dorian Gray, rather than just a brute.

But then, the classic "monster tales" are connected in lots of ways. In Mary Shelley's *Frankenstein*, Victor Frankenstein compares his creation to both a vampire and an animated mummy. Frankenstein's Monster and the vampire, since 1816, have often been twinned in popular culture. It almost seems as though the "Monster Mash" was preordained. But that's the nature of archetypes; they capture something so deep in our "collective unconscious" that they seem inevitable. The same can be said of such nonhorror archetypes as Sherlock Holmes and Superman.

Bram Stoker, Irish-born manager of the great English actor, Sir Henry Irving, did copious research into vampire lore. He also was influenced, if only slightly, by tales of the real historical fiend, Vlad Tepes (1431?-1476), known as Dracula, "son of the Devil." Unlike most of his film adaptations, the Count Dracula of Stoker's novel was aggressive and repulsive, undead. (More monster-mixing: Stoker's Dracula was a werewolf as well as a vampire, a detail given only passing film attention until Francis Ford Coppola's 1992 adaptation.) The suave, seductive figure of most Dracula films borrows from Polidori's romantic, Byronic vampire.

To add still more doubling, Skal points out that Stoker and Wilde both grew up in Dublin, and young Wilde (before discovering that he was gay) courted Florence Balcolme, whom Stoker later married. Wilde's life ended in tragic scandal. Stoker continued to present a figure of stiff Victorian respectability. But, while lacking Wilde's wit and his conscious artistry, Stoker had an inner life as complex as Wilde's. Stoker poured into his magnum opus oceans of unconscious concerns about Victorian culture and its repressed sexuality, making *Dracula* the most memorably lurid novel of the late nineteenth century. (Other Stoker works that have inspired films are the giant-serpent novel, *The Lair of the White Worm*, 1911, and the thrice-filmed mummy novel, *The Jewel of the Seven Stars*, 1903.)

Again meanwhile, as popular magazines appeared and grew, mystery and detective fiction also flourished in the hands of such masters as Poe and Sir Arthur Conan Doyle (1859-1930). Sometimes mysteries shaded into horror, notably in Poe's "The Murders in the Rue Morgue" (1841) and Conan Doyle's Sherlock Holmes novel, *The Hound of the Baskervilles* (1902). Conan Doyle, a storyteller of unsurpassed range, wrote nearly every kind of popular fiction, including the thrice-filmed science fiction dinosaur adventure, *The Lost World*, (1912), and several supernatural yarns, including two mummy stories, "Lot No. 249" and "The Ring of Thoth," that almost certainly influenced the classic mummy films. And proto-science fiction developed out of Shelley, Poe, and Hawthorne into the "Voyages Extraordinaire" of French novelist Jules Verne (1828-1905) and the "scientific romances" of England's H.G. Wells (1866-1946). Verne, prior to his dark novel *Master of the World* (1904), tended to be a booster of science and technology, but Wells in his best work took a more cautionary tone, and some of these tales, especially *The Island of Dr. Moreau* (1896) and *The Invisible Man* (1897) partook strongly of horror. Both were brilliantly filmed in the '30s.

In 1897, the Grand Guignol theater opened in Paris, featuring horror plays with extremely graphic stage violence, and remained open until 1964. (David J. Skal has suggested that the Grand Guignol may have survived the Occupation of the 1940s because Hermann Goering had a taste for its horrors.)

Due to "persistence of vision," by which images linger on the retina for a fraction of a second, rapidly switching similar pictures cause the eye to see a continuous moving image. Various devices have used this principle to provide entertainment simulating motion; in 1790s Paris, the *Fantasmagorie* "magic lantern" shows projected eerie gothic horror images. In 1888, the Eastman Kodak company began marketing portable cameras using celluloid film. The next year, William Kennedy Dickson at Edison Studios invented the first real motion picture camera, the kinetoscope, using a celluloid filmstrip, because Edison wanted a visual companion to his 1877 invention, the phonograph. But synchronization of sound and pictures remained out of reach. Edison, failing to see the potential of theatrical films, came up with a boxy device that let one person view the images at a time. Kinetoscope-viewing parlors started up in 1894, using Edison Studios films of gags, boxing kangaroos, and human performances running from a few seconds to a minute. In 1895, France's Lumiere (French for "light") brothers patented the cinematographe, a portable sixteen pound combination film camera, film printer, and projector.

In December 1895, the Lumiere brothers invited noted stage magician George Melies (1861-1938) to an early showing of the cinematographe. Afire with the potential of moving pictures, Melies attempted to purchase a cinematographe from the Lumieres, who, smelling competition, turned him down. He bought a British motion picture camera, analyzed it, designed his own, the kinetographe, and began showing short films (a minute and up) between magic bits in his own magic theater, the Robert-Houdin. At first, he imitated the straight reproduction of everyday scenes. Indeed, he pioneered the "reconstructed newsreel," filmed reenactments of recent news events. But Melies was, first and foremost, a magician, and he felt constrained by reproducing mundane reality. One day in 1896, his camera jammed, skipped a few frames, and he was amazed, watching his film of a city street, to see a bus "turn into" a hearse. Trick photography, long a feature of still photos, was reborn in movies.

Melies built his own movie studio (the second in the world, after Edison's) out of glass walls, in his garden in Montreuil, France. He devised, directed, and usually starred in increasingly elaborate short films. The three-minute *The Devil's Castle* (1896), the first horror film, shows a bat turning into Mephistopheles. Mephistopheles conjures up a ghost, witches, and a skeleton, then disappears in a puff of smoke at the sight of a cross. All this the year before Stoker's *Dracula*! Many of Melies' films featured fantastic story lines, including *The Laboratory of Mephistopheles* (1897), which made the Devil films' first mad scientist, *The Astronomer's Dream, or the Man in the Moon* (1898), and *Cinderella* (seven minutes, 1899).

A Trip to the Moon (fourteen minutes, 1902), generally considered his masterpiece, is the first science fiction film, combining and spoofing elements of *From the Earth to the Moon* by Verne and *The First Men in the Moon* by Wells. It remains great fun. You've probably seen its most famous image—as the rocket from Earth lands on the Moon, we see the Man in the Moon licking his lips in pain, the rocket protruding from his eye. We also see women in classical garb representing the constellations, and acrobats from the Folies-Bergere as the hopping Selenites. It should be pointed out that the first major film Western, Edwin S. Porter's *The Great Train Robbery*, premiered the next year

(1903). It used to be fashionable for critics to diss genre films, and the members of the Academy of Motion Picture Arts and Sciences still overlook them today. But genrefication is as old as narrative film.

Other Melies fantasies include *An Impossible Voyage* (twenty four minutes, 1904), featuring trips to the Sun's surface and the ocean's bottom, and *The Conquest of the Pole* (1912). Many of his other films employ what we would now call surrealism (though they preceded that post-WWI literary and art movement), as objects, without rhyme or reason, turn into people, then back into objects. Most of Melies' films are comedies, eschewing overt horror, but his reality-twists, especially his plastic use of the human figure, can be disturbing. *The Conquest of the Pole* also features a monster, the Giant of the Snows, who swallows, then regurgitates, members of a polar expedition.

Melies invented or polished much of the language of film, including the dissolve and slow and fast motion. Gradually, though, his films fell out of fashion. His film studio, Star Films, went out of business in 1913, and he was forced to sell his magic theater in 1925. He was a magician who loved using movies to make magic; he had less regard for storytelling as such, saying, "You could say that the scenario is in this case simply a thread intended to link the 'effects'…I was appealing to the spectator's eyes alone, trying to charm and intrigue him, hence the scenario was of no importance."

The traditional rap is that Melies, the inventor of narrative cinema, failed to fully make the transition from FX for the sake of FX to FX enhancing a story. (It's hard for me to resist thinking that when contemporary filmmakers abandon story logic and consistent characterization to wallow in FX, they're recapitulating the major misstep of the first film director.) The other traditional criticism of Melies is that, though many of his magics remain impressive a century later, they are stage magics. He didn't move his camera much.

But, in *Marvelous Melies*, Paul Hammond makes a spirited case for the defense. He argues that, for Melies, the tricks were the thing; that in asking for stronger story lines, critics unfairly bash him for "failing" to do something he wasn't trying to do, and that Melies knowingly kept the camera static to put us in a state of reverie, receptive to his marvelous transformations. (Accepted on his own terms, Melies can be enjoyed in much the way the zany surrealism in *Monty Python's Flying Circus* can be enjoyed.) Hammond writes, "Far from being obsolete, George Melies' vision is full of promise."

After a difficult late middle age selling candy and toys, Melies lived to see his work rediscovered. Though they remained poor, he and his wife were given a free apartment by the French film industry, and he received a number of visits from people eager to meet cinema's great pioneer.

In the U.S., the first brief film of *Dr. Jekyll and Mr. Hyde* occurred in 1908; a 16-? minute Edison Studios *Frankenstein* came out in 1910. For the latter, the creation of the monster was depicted by burning a dummy, then

A Trip to the Moon (1902)

running the film backward. A private collector has recently released clips of that film; a 1915 U.S. *Frankenstein* adaptation, *Life Without Soul*, remains lost. D.W. Griffith made "The Tell-Tale Heart" and bits of other Poe stories and poems into a full-length film, *The Avenging Conscience* (1914), which has been described as the first American horror masterpiece.

But as with fiction, so with film: the tale of terror flowered in Germany before taking proper root in the U.S. In 1913 came the German-made *The Student of Prague*. Writer Hanns Heinz Ewers, borrowing elements from Hoffman, Poe, and Wilde, scripted a film about a man (Paul Wegener) who makes a demonic bargain that gives birth to his evil mirror-*doppelganger*.

While the film was being shot on location in Prague, Wegener (1874-1948), figuratively and literally a giant of the German stage, learned of the Jewish legend of golems, clay statues supposedly endowed with life by cabalistic magic, and one particularly famous Golem brought to life by sixteenth century Prague's Rabbi Loew. Wegener was probably also aware of Bavarian writer Gustav Meyrink's novel, *The Golem* (serialized 1913). Wegener, as co-writer, director, and star, used the figure of the Golem in three films. In *The Golem* (1915) the Golem (Wegener) is unearthed in twentieth century Prague and an antique dealer revives him, with disastrous results. *The Golem and the Dancing Girl* (1917) may have been a comedy.

These films appear to be lost; but *The Golem: How He Came into the World* (1920) survives. It is one of the first movie prequels, set in sixteenth century Prague whose Jewish community is threatened by a pogrom from the emperor. Rabbi Loew—who is at once portrayed as a devoutly religious man, a scientist scanning the heavens with a telescope, and a magician with incantations and pointed hat—resolves to build a golem to save his people. In an impressively imaginative scene, he summons the demon Astaroth, compelling the demon to reveal the word that will bring his clay statue to life (we see the letters of the word—aemet—emerging from Astaroth's mouth.) In an audience with the emperor, the Golem saves the emperor's life, causing the emperor to rescind his edict against the Jews. But the Golem is later used by others for selfish purposes, and the Golem goes out of control.

Wegener's 1920 *Golem* clearly influenced director James Whale's 1931 *Frankenstein.* Both creatures are massive, clumsy, essentially mute. (The Monster makes animal noises.) *The Golem* includes a scene in which the clay man encounters a little girl who approaches him, innocent of fear—a scene to which Whale would pay direct homage in *Frankenstein.* (Still more monster- doubling: the connection between *Frankenstein* and the Golem might go back to 1816, since there could easily have been a golem tale or two in that book of German ghost stories at Lake Geneva.) The 1920 *Golem*, like its namesake, is a slow-moving film, but a handsome one. Especially impressive are the sets constructed by architect Hans Poelzig, including a ghetto of fifty-four plaster houses connected by twisting streets. Wegener's restrained performance gives his Golem dignity, as his slow movements emphasize the Golem's great mass, power, and potential menace. And Wegener's Golem, like Karloff's Monster, yearns to be loved, real.

An aspect of Mary Shelley's *Frankenstein* that puzzles contemporary readers is why Victor Frankenstein, who had eagerly anticipated making a living man, recoils in horror when his creation actually comes to life. Nineteenth century readers understood that Frankenstein is shocked at the "wrongness"

of seeing a being animated by other than "natural" means. In the 1990s, crowds of villagers with torches didn't riot over the cloning of Dolly the sheep partly because we've had seven decades of Boris Karloff's sympathetic performance as The Monster. But the horror of "unnatural" creation kept coming up in silent German cinema. The six-part serial *Homunculus* (1916), chronicles a laboratory-created man (Olaf Fonss) who, though brilliant and handsome, is rejected by people—especially women he courts—when they learn he's artificial. In a plot line that now seems prescient, he goes mad, becomes a dictator, and starts a world war. Finally he's struck down with a lightning bolt. Another approach to unnatural creation was Hanns Heinz Ewers' 1911 novel, *Alraune*, about a soulless woman, created through artificial insemination, who ruins the lives of those who love her. Germans

Paul Wegener and "girl with apple" in
The Golem (1920)

filmed it several times, most successfully in 1928 with Brigitte Helm and Wegener.

From 1919-1933 post-WW I Germany had its first democratic government, the Weimar Republic (an experiment ended when Hitler was elected Chancellor with 44 percent of the vote in a three-way race, a fact I delight in pointing out to self-indulgent idiots who say voting doesn't matter). During the Weimar period, Germany produced a number of its best-remembered films. Several films of 1919-1924, especially, reflected Germany's postwar economic depression in their dark-fantastic tone.

In 1919, two young men, Carl Mayer and Hans Janowitz, persuaded Erich Pommer of the Decla Film Company to produce their screenplay, *The Cabinet of Dr. Caligari*; Pommer hired Robert Wiene to direct. It was the strange story of a carnival sideshowman, Dr. Caligari (Werner Krauss), who exhibits a cadaverous somnambulist (sleepwalker) named Cesare (Conrad Veidt—pronounced "Vite"—1893-1943). At night Caligari sends Cesare out to commit murders. The young hero, Francis (Friedrich Peher), suspecting that Caligari is behind the murders, goes to the local asylum to see if they have a patient named Caligari, only to learn that the insane Caligari is the asylum director! Mayer and Janowitz, bitter about Germany's recent participation in World War I, intended *Caligari* as a criticism of authority figures in general. They were aghast when Wiene and Pommer changed the narrative frame of the story to make it the ravings of the insane Francis, who only believes that the apparently benign asylum director (Krauss) is Caligari. This frame seemed to undercut the writers' intentions by affirming authority. But *The Cabinet of Dr. Caligari* (1920) was a revolutionary film in a different way—through its use of expressionism.

Expressionism was a school of art and writing that eschewed surface realism, emphasizing the underlying emotional tone of things. Important impressionist painters included Henri Matisse (1869-1954) and Edvard Munch (1863-1944). Munch (whose most famous painting, *The Scream*, 1893, inspired the serial-killer mask in a popular trilogy of late-twentieth century American films) was hired by the head of the German Theater, Max Reinhardt, to help design the sets for his theater's first production in 1906. Reinhardt, though not an expressionist per se, made sophisticated theatrical use of light and shadow to convey mood. Paul Wegener, Werner Krauss, and Konrad Veidt all acted in his *kammerspiele* (intimate theater), and Hans Poelzig designed another theater for Reinhardt. The "expressionist" label has been applied to most of the Weimar-period German films mentioned in this column, but especially to *Caligari*.

Caligari's painted sets helped save money—painted shadows reduced the need for electricity—while giving *Caligari* a look that no other film has ever duplicated. Like expressionist paintings, the sets sheer off at odd angles (there may also be an element of cubism in the sets' distortion). The backdrops of the film, suggestive of the psychological disturbance of the characters, gave a very odd look to an odd story. It is even possible to argue whether the narrative frame succeeds in undermining the screenwriters' intent. The landscapes are still in place at film's end, even though we're presumably back in the "real" world. And the look on the face of the psychiatrist who claims not to be Caligari as he resolves to cure his patient is a tad ambiguous. Just as the 1956 *Invasion of the Body Snatchers* is a paranoid masterpiece despite its studio-mandated happy ending, so one comes away from *Caligari* with a vision of society off-kilter, much as the writers intended.

Only Veidt and Krauss, stage veterans familiar with expressionist theater, appear to have sensed that *Caligari*'s story and sets called for stylized acting. The more conventional performances are forgettable, yet we vividly recall Krauss' demented grandiloquence, and Veidt's balletic movements. Siegfried Kracauer wrote that when Veidt's Cesare "prowled along a wall, it was as if the wall exuded him." In horror, it's mainly the grand characters that we remember.

Caligari's fascination is mainly a painterly fascination—as a filmed story, it's relatively static, a weakness that critics noted even in the '20s. But considered as a waking dream, it succeeds very well, and in some ways anticipates the films of David Lynch.

In any case, this respected and influential film lent weight to the Melies position—that films need not simply photograph realistic surfaces, but may occur in wholly imaginary settings. It's also worth noting that Caligari's sending of his "monster" out to commit acts of mayhem prefigures Universal's *Son* (1939) and *Ghost* (1942) and Hammer's *Evil of Frankenstein* (1964). And Veidt's somnambulist, like Karloff's Monster—and unlike so many recent film psycho-killers—is a strange person, but a person. Cesare is told to kill the female lead (Lil Dagover), but he resists, even though his resistance leads to his death. Too, the figure of Cesare, clad in head-to-foot black leotard, lying in a coffin-like box, most likely influenced many a vampire film.

Another important 1920 German film, now lost, was *Der Januskopf* (*The Head of Janus*), loosely adapted by Hans Janowitz from *Dr. Jekyll and Mr. Hyde*, starring Conrad Veidt as "Dr. Warren" and "Mr. O'Connor," and featuring a thirty-something Hungarian stage actor named Bela Lugosi as Dr.

Conrad Veidt and Lil Dagover in
The Cabinet of Dr. Caligari (1920)

Warren's butler. The film marked the directorial debut of F.W. Murnau (1888-1930). Supernatural vampires had so far had little screen time: the terms "vamp" and "vampire" were used in films to describe non-supernatural predatory women. And, surprisingly, Bram Stoker hadn't managed to generate a stage play of *Dracula* during his lifetime. But in 1921, businessman Enrico Dieckmann and artist Albin Grau formed Prana Film, planning an adaptation of *Dracula* as the studio's first film. Grau served, with great distinction, as the film's production designer, and they hired Murnau to direct and Henrik Galeen to script (Murnau and Galeen, too, had worked with Max Reinhardt). In hopes of avoiding copyright problems, the title was changed from *Dracula* to *Nosferatu: A Symphony of Horror*, the characters' names were changed (Dracula became Count Orlok), and the main setting switched from late-nineteenth century London to Bremen, Germany in 1838. But the plot, though greatly stripped down, was fairly close to that of Stoker's novel, including some of the novel's most memorable scenes, such as the ship whose crew the vampire has killed sailing into harbor with the dead captain roped to the steering wheel.

Nosferatu's pace is mostly fast—when it slows down, it slows down to good, eerie effect—and the photography is inventive. Though Stoker's Dracula cast no shadows, Nosferatu casts some spooky ones (Coppola made amusing homage to this in his 1992 *Dracula*). Most important, Orlok/Nosferatu /Dracula (Max Schreck, 1879-1936) was, and remains, a genuinely creepy monster. Though differing in detail from the white-haired-and-mustached Count of Stoker's novel, Nosferatu is similar in spirit—a walking corpse. He is the lord of rats, whose arrival by ship in Bremen brings rats and the plague, and he himself resembles a human vermin. Indeed, he *is* the plague, for with his death the plague departs.

Nina Harker, or Ellen Hutter, depending on your print of the film (Greta Schroder), in what was probably the first substantive female role in a horror film, has psychic intimations of the vampire's menace to Bremen in general and her husband in particular. She sacrifices herself by offering herself freely to the vampire, keeping him by her bedside until the break of dawn, when he dissolves, like a nightmare, at the sunlight's touch. This scene is the origin of the tradition that sunlight kills vampires. In Stoker, Dracula mostly avoided daylight, because it reduced his powers, making him vulnerable, but he could go out by day if he needed to. While kulcha-snobs may have a snit about this, it seems to me that film, a people's art, is a valid participant in the folklore process.

Most of the Weimar fantastic films were filmed in-studio, giving the filmmakers control of their environments—but *Nosferatu* made extensive and striking use of on-location outdoor photography in Central Europe. Murnau knew how to use nature to enhance his desired moods. Of all the German silents discussed here, *Nosferatu* remains the creepiest, and (easily) the most fun.

Alas, Grau & co.'s business sense was not equal to their storytelling, and *Nosferatu*, released in 1922, was Prana Film's only production. And, in a comedy of manners detailed by Skal in *Hollywood Gothic*, Florence Stoker sued them for infringement of her late husband's copyright, and when it became clear that no royalties would be forthcoming, she sought the destruction of all copies of the film. While she was well within her legal rights, and Prana Film did wrong by adapting *Dracula* without her permission, we may rightly celebrate the fact that a few pirated copies survived of a great film that does her husband proud.

Other important German films of the early-to-mid-'20s featuring fantastic content included the technically ambitious *Warning Shadows* (1923), whose main action is a play performed by animated shadows, and *Waxworks* (1924), the first film of director Paul Leni, in which a man makes up stories about a carnival's wax figures, including Ivan the Terrible (Conrad Veidt) and Jack the Ripper (Werner Krauss). *The Hands of Orlac* (1925), directed by Robert Wiene from a novel by Maurice Renaud, starred Veidt as Orlac, a pianist who has his hands amputated after a railroad accident and replaced with those of a murderer. When a series of murders occurs, Orlac suspects that his hands are doing the killings. *Orlac* would be remade twice, notably in the U.S. as *Mad Love* (1935). Henrik Galeen directed a

Max Schreck in
Die Nosferatu (1922)

remake of *The Student of Prague* (1926), with Veidt as the student and Werner Krauss as the Devil. Murnau directed a version of the deal-with-the-Devil legend, *Faust* (1926).

No survey of silent German films would be complete without mentioning the early career of Fritz Lang (pronounced "long"— 1890-1976). Born in Vienna, he studied to be a builder like his father, but ran away from home at twenty. By the time he started directing films in 1919, he had traveled widely, sold sketches in Paris, been a decorated veteran in the Austrian army, an actor, fiction writer, screenplay writer, and film story-editor. An early directorial success was *The Spiders* (1919-20), an exotic serial about a crime syndicate. In the '20s, he collaborated on several films with his screenwriter wife,

Thea Von Harbou (1888-1954), including *Destiny* (1921) involving a bargain with Death personified, and *Dr. Mabuse, the Gambler* (1922), a dark thriller about a criminal mastermind. They made a big-budget, two-part adaptation of the German epic, *The Nibelungen: Siegfried* and *Kriemheld's Revenge* (both 1924). These could have been ponderous, but Lang was a born storyteller. *Siegfried* is a ripping fantasy adventure with a dragon, dwarf's treasure, and foul betrayal, and *Kriemheld's Revenge* is a fascinatingly grim tale of Siegfried's wife sacrificing all to avenge her murdered husband. The Nibelung films were such a success that Lang and Von Harbou were pretty much given a blank check for their next film.

Metropolis (1927), the first masterpiece of science fiction cinema, about an early twenty-first century city based on Manhattan, was controversial on its release and remains so three generations later. Its story line and philosophical content are still praised as far-sighted and still dismissed as simplistic and sentimental. Dr. David Soren points out that Lang's blocklike city was designed in criticism of Bauhaus architecture's standardized housing units (which have also become commonplace in American suburbia). And Lang's portrayal of irrational, easily influenced crowds may seem unreal, but they proved all too close a prediction of what actually happened in Germany a few years after the film's release.

The images of a machine society that dehumanizes its workers linger in the mind of anyone who's seen the film, especially the scene in which a man's arms function like a clock's arms in the operation of a machine. Several times, at intervals of several years, I've gone to see the film dutifully, expecting it to be ponderous, only to find myself pleasantly swept away by what remains, whatever its failings, a great story. There's that magnificent city, which would influence dark science fiction cities in *Blade Runner* (1982), *Dark City* (1997) and other films. There's the succession of grand scenes. As in *Caligari*, it's the fantastical characters who remain fresh: Rotwang (Rudolf Klein-Rogge) the prototype of all future mad scientists, and his evil female robot (Brigitte Helm). The scene in which the robot, surrounded by hoops of light, turns into the doppelganger of Maria the virtuous labor agitator (also Brigitte Helm) remains one of the most vivid scenes in fantastic cinema.

Lang was criticized for the film's anti-technological tone, so he made *The Woman in the Moon* (1929), in consultation with scientist Wiley Ley—a state-of-the-art speculation about how humans could travel to the Moon. The human story now seems contrived, but the science holds up remarkably well.

As real shadows lengthened over Germany in the late '20s and early '30s, several of the talents who had made the first coherent body of film horror left Germany for Hollywood. Directors Paul Leni and W.F. Murnau both had short, brilliant Hollywood careers before dying tragically young. For example, Leni would make the American thriller *The Cat and the Canary* (1927), which, though non-supernatural, set the look for "haunted house" films; and Murnau directed Veidt in an adaptation of Victor Hugo's horrific human story of a man with a frozen smile, *The Man Who Laughs* (1928). Hungarian director Michael Curtiz hadn't directed horror films while working in Germany, but made several good ones in the U.S., including *The Mystery of the Wax Museum* (1933) and *The Walking Dead* (1936), as well as directing *Casablanca* (1942). Karl Freund (1890-1969), who had served as photographer on the 1920 *Golem* and on *Metropolis* (1927), would photograph fellow immigrant Lugosi in Tod Browning's *Dracula* (1931), and would himself direct Karloff in *The Mummy* (1932) and fellow-immigrant Lorre in *Mad Love* (1935). Edgar G. Ulmer, an assistant director to Murnau, went on to direct the expressionist horror classic, *The Black Cat* (1934). Scriptwriter Curt Siodmak wrote several U.S. horror films, most notably *The Wolf Man* (1941). Musician Franz Waxman scored many U.S. films, including the magnificent score for *Bride of Frankenstein* (1935).

Lang followed *M* with a "Mabuse" sequel, *The Testament of Dr. Mabuse* (1933), in which Mabuse dies in an insane asylum but his ghost seems to take possession of the asylum's director. The insane Mabuse also spouts Nazi slogans. The film was suppressed by the new Nazi regime (though a crew member smuggled it to France), and, sometime in 1933, Lang wound up in Paris. Lang, who loved a good story, perhaps compressed a series of incidents into one day. Lang said that Nazi Minister of Propaganda Joseph Goebbels summoned him to his office, where Goebbels apologized for pulling *Mabuse* but said that he and Hitler admired Lang's work and wanted to appoint him head of the German cinema. Lang said that he told Goebbels he'd consider the offer, then caught the night train to

Gustav Froelich, Rudolf Klein-Rogge, and Brigitte Helm in *Metropolis* (1927)

Paris. Whether or not it happened that way, Lang eventually made his way to Hollywood, where he directed nearly every genre of film. Conrad Veidt, a gentile who, in solidarity with his Jewish wife, had been courageously listing himself as "Juden" on German forms, went on, in England and the U.S., to be a symbol of resistance to Nazism, and to play Major Strasser in *Casablanca*.

Of the silent films discussed, I've seen *A Trip to the Moon, The Conquest of the Pole, The Golem, The Cabinet of Dr. Caligari, Nosferatu, Siegfried, Kriemheld's Revenge, Metropolis, and The Woman in the Moon* (as well as several of Lang's sound films), and have learned that several others are available commercially, including *The Avenging Conscience*, both versions of *The Student of Prague, The Spiders, Destiny, Dr. Mabuse: The Gambler, Warning Shadows, Waxworks*, and *The Hands of Orlac*. But why watch them?

First, because history matters, our disposable U.S. culture notwithstanding. When released these were, mostly, seen as major films, intimately connected to the theatrical, literary, and art movements of the time. They were criticized, but in the way that major films are criticized. *Caligari* stirred up a sensation, first throughout Europe, then in the U.S. From the '20s to the mid-'30s. A-picture status would also be accorded to such American films as *The Phantom of the Opera, Dracula, Frankenstein, Dr. Jekyll and Mr. Hyde, King Kong*, and *Bride of Frankenstein*. In the magic of Melies and the terrors of Germany, we see the language being written and the groundwork laid for American horror's Golden Age, just as Golden Age horror would sharpen and refine the language for the films to follow.

Second, but equally important, these silent European films are fascinating in their own right, if we stretch ourselves to appreciate them. Silent films do have a very differ-

ent idiom from what we're accustomed to. Most of them require extra concentration, and more than one viewing, just to get their plots, let alone to pick up on subtleties. But, as with other durable artworks, if we give more of ourselves to them, we get more back.

Sources: Since 1964, I've read uncountable books and articles on classic horror. In direct preparation for this column I'm indebted to John D. Barlow, *German Expressionist Film* (1982); Peter Bogdanovich, interview with Fritz Lang in *Who the Devil Made it* (1997); Carlos Clarens, *An Illustrated History of the Horror Film* (1967); David A. Cook, *A History of Narrative Film* (1981); Lotte Eisner, *The Haunted Screen: Expressionism in the German Cinema and the Influence of Max Reinhardt* (1969), *Murnau* (1973), and *Fritz Lang* (1986); Paul Hammond, *Marvelous Melies* (1974); Boris Karloff, ed., *Tales of Terror* (1943); Ephraim Katz, *The Film Encyclopedia* (1979); Siegfried Kracauer, *From Caligari to Hitler: A Psychological History of the German Film* (1947); Dr. Patrick McGilligan, *Fritz Lang: Nature of the Beast* (1997); Roger Maxwell, ed., *Masterworks of the German Cinema* (1973); David J. Skal, *Hollywood Gothic: The Tangled Web of Dracula from Novel to Stage to Screen* (1990), *The Monster Show: A Cultural History of Horror* (1994), and *Screams of Reason: Mad Science and Modern Culture* (1998); and Dr. David Soren, *The Rise and Fall of the Horror Film* (1995); as well as these Internet sources: *The Internet Movie Database; LSVideo*; Diane MacIntyre's *The Silents Majority* web article on "Horror Films;" *The Metropolis Home Page*; the *Silent Thrills* website with its assorted links, especially, D. Honigsberg's essay, "Rava's Golem;" and *The Conrad Veidt Home Page*, where you can hear Veidt sing "When the Lighthouse Shines Across the Bay."

SUBMISSION GUIDELINES

Fiction: Payment 3¢ per word for literate speculative fiction. This includes science fiction, fantasy, horror, magic realism, literary, and especially unclassifiable stories that blur the boundaries of all of these designations, up to 8,000 words. See the editorial at the beginning of this magazine for a description of the sort of fiction we're looking for, then read the stories. Readers of *Darkling Plain* care less about genre distinctions and more about a good story, well told. If you can do that, your chances are pretty good with us.

Response time will be two to six weeks. I may take longer if the story is under consideration, so wait two months before querying.

And now, a word about editorial responses: I will try to respond personally to most manuscript submissions, even if it's only a sentence or two. On the other hand, if I have something to say about the story, I may respond with quite a few sentences. One of the goals of a good editor is to help writers improve their story and their craft, and that sometimes means being critical. If you can't appreciate criticism, grow a thicker skin, because any successful writer will tell you they received a lot of criticism on the way to success, at which point they received plenty more. It's worse when nobody says anything at all. If you take the time to submit your best work, I look forward to letting you know what I thought.

Poetry: $25 for speculative poetry, up to two typewritten pages per poem.

Nonfiction: Payment 3¢ per word for critical essays on writers, themes, and works of speculative fiction—including original work that has appeared in *Darkling Plain*—and speculative science articles, to 5,000 words. Interviews 1-3¢ per word.

Illustrations and Cartoons: $60.00 for front cover art, $35 for back-cover art, and $25 for commissioned interior art. For an assignment, please send clear, disposable samples of your work first. DO NOT send originals unless requested.

Reading for issue #2 from May 1, 2000 to July 1, 2000. Please do not submit any material other than these times, as it might be quite a while before I am able to respond.

Send all submissions to:

Darkling Plain
4804 Laurel Canyon Blvd
Box 506
Valley Village CA 91607

Darkling Plain and its editor assume no responsibility for unsolicited manuscripts. If you want your manuscript returned to you, include a SASE with sufficient postage, and remember that the Post Office determines what constitutes sufficient postage. Manuscripts without an SASE will not be returned. Postage-due submissions of any sort will be refused. If you include an e-mail address with your submission and advise me that you do not need your manuscript returned, no SASE is necessary—I'll respond via e-mail.

9 781929 611140